THE GOVERNESS CLUB: BONNIE

By Ellie Macdonald

The Governess Club: Claire
The Governess Club: Bonnie

THE GOVERNESS
CLUB: BONNIE

ELLIE MACDONALD

AVONIMPULSE
An Imprint of HarperCollinsPublishers

Excerpt from *Skies of Gold* copyright © 2013 by Zoë Archer.

Excerpt from *Crave* copyright © 2013 by Karen Erickson.

Excerpt from *Can't Help Falling in Love* copyright © 2013 by Cheryl Harper.

Excerpt from *Things Good Girls Don't Do* copyright © 2013 by Codi Gary.

EPub Edition SEPTEMBER 2013 ISBN: 9780062292247

Print Edition ISBN: 9780062292254

JV 10 9 8 7 6 5 4 3 2 1

CHAPTER ONE

My dearest Claire,

Felicitations on your betrothal to Mr. Knightly. I am simply overjoyed for you, for there is no one more deserving of happiness than you. Does he by any chance have an unmarried brother you can mention me to? I am almost too embarrassed to admit how much I giggled at my pitiful joke. We are in much need of levity at Darrowgate these days.

I sincerely wish that I could be with you during the planning of your wedding. I simply cannot justify leaving my charges at this time. The upheaval that would be caused by my departure, so soon after the tragedy that claimed their parents, would devastate them. Henry walks around for all appearances an old man with the weight of the world on his shoulders; a younger, more solemn viscount I have not seen. And Arthur—poor Arthur. He continues to cling to me; we have not heard him utter a sound since that day and his thumb sucking returned shortly after the funeral.

There is more, however, and I can feel my cheeks heat with indignant anger just thinking about it. I have oft heard the term "fair-weather friend" but had yet to experience it. Indeed, I feel ashamed to be placed in the same category as these people, as I am sure you, Sara, and Louisa will as well.

The servants have been abandoning Darrowgate— abandoning Henry and Arthur, if I am to be blunt. The guardian chosen in the late Viscount Darrow's will has yet to arrive and Mr. Renard refuses to release any money to pay wages on the grounds that it exceeds his authority. Exceeds his authority, indeed! For more years that I have been a governess here, the man of business has always paid out the servants' wages. Several of the maids here send money home to their families; I know the stable master has a wife and three young mouths to feed, and he is only one of many in such a situation. Exceeds his authority, indeed!

With this in mind, can I truly blame the servants for leaving an uncertain prospect? Part of me does. Have they no loyalty to Henry or Arthur? Or to the viscountcy? Most have been here longer than I and yet they have fled at the first sign of trouble. How can a boy of eight years be expected to manage a household? I am not sure which angers me more: their disloyalty to the viscountcy or their callous abandonment of two young children entirely unprepared for life as orphans. Has honor and integrity disappeared amongst the servant class?

I must be completely honest with you, dearest Claire; even from this distance I can feel your steady gaze on me, silently asking me questions and patiently waiting for me to answer. Your concerns are not unfounded. I have not fully recovered from the incident either. There are times when I wake in the middle of the night hearing the screams of the horses mix with those of Viscount and Viscountess Darrow. Have you ever noticed how similar the sounds of screaming humans and horses are? And at times the memory of the coach mangling before me is so real I fear I could touch it. Even now, the sound of a coach approaching paralyzes me. I refuse to force the boys to ride in one, but I wonder if that is more for my sake than theirs.

Of course I am aware that recovery is likely to be quicker away from Darrowgate, but I refuse to abandon Henry and Arthur in their present condition, even if I were not suffering my present abhorrence of coaches. Remaining here until the guardian arrives will be best for everyone, I believe. Hopefully the wait will not be much longer; it has already been over a month since the accident.

Please convey my regrets to Louisa and Sara for not being able to fulfill my part of the Governess Club at this time, but as I described, present circumstances are not ideal. I do beg you, however, please do not mention my own struggles. I would not wish any of you to concern yourself with this. There is much to occupy yourselves with your wedding and establishing our club's reputation. I will recover; it is only a matter of time.

I miss all of you, my dear friends and sisters.

> With all my love,
> Bonnie

CHAPTER TWO

October 1822

Bonnie looked down at the blond boy walking next to her and pasted on a confident smile. "I am sure next time we will have more success."

Henry glanced at her, but did not smile or share her enthusiasm. "It's too late in the year, I think. It's a poor time to fish." He shifted the two poles he carried to the other shoulder. "And the worms are difficult to find. You said that they burrow deeper into the ground the colder it gets."

"That is true," Bonnie conceded. "But I do not think it is so cold that they will be hibernating just yet. They will be deeper, yes, but earthworms do not fully enter hibernation until it is almost freezing."

"I remember," Henry replied.

"Besides, it will simply mean that we have to dig a bit deeper," Bonnie said with forced cheerfulness. "How about that, Arthur? Would you like to dig deeper holes in the garden?" She gave the three-year-old's hand a squeeze. He just looked at her with solemn brown eyes.

"Mother does not like us ruining her garden," Henry said

quietly. "Father said it's best to dig at night when she can't see us. The deeper holes would not please my mother."

Bonnie closed her eyes and bit back a sigh. "My lord, I do not think your mother would begrudge you worms for fishing."

Henry said, "Still, I would rather not."

The trio crested the hill and Darrowgate came into view. The house, granted with the viscountcy by King Henry VII, was in the tribute shape of an *H*. As they drew closer, the large red stone building imposed itself on the landscape, a testament to the legacy of the Darrows.

Bonnie led the boys through the garden; Henry kept his stoic eyes on the house and Arthur removed his thumb from his mouth long enough to trail his fingers on the flowers in late bloom. By the time they had climbed the four small steps to the terrace, the thumb was firmly back in place.

"Burdis," Henry called the butler as they entered the main hall from the rear. "Please inform Mrs. Dabbs that there will be no fish complimenting dinner tonight." He handed the poles to the portly man.

"Of course, my lord. Better luck next time. Hodges," Burdis turned his steady gaze to Bonnie. "There is a gentleman waiting in the drawing room. His name is Montgomery."

Bonnie was curious. "For me?"

"He asked for the viscount." Burdis lowered his voice. "He does not seem aware of the recent change. They were friends."

"Oh." Bonnie was startled. She took a deep breath and looked down at Henry. "Shall we greet this visitor, my lord?"

Henry regarded her with solemn eyes. "You don't need to address me like that. I am still Henry."

Bonnie knelt down to his level. "You know well enough that you are the viscount. It is proper. You had best get used to it."

"As the viscount, I insist you address me as you always have, as Henry." He looked at Burdis. "And for the other servants to call you Miss Hodges."

The butler inclined his head in acknowledgment. Bonnie gave Henry a weak smile and smoothed his coat lapels. "Mr. Montgomery is waiting." At Henry's nod, they moved to the drawing room, Arthur's hand in hers, his older brother with shoulders squared and chin raised.

Mr. Montgomery looked up at their entrance, his hands stretched towards the fire, warming his fingers. Seeing them, he turned and moved across the room, his eyes sharp as he looked them over. He stopped in front of Henry.

"Henry," he said, his voice infused with a Scottish burr. "You have grown. Do you remember me?"

Henry didn't answer. Glancing down at him, Bonnie could see his throat working as though he was trying to force a sound out of his mouth. She rested a hand on his shoulder and felt his paralysis.

The man looked to the other boy. "Arthur, is it?" The younger boy buried his head in Bonnie's skirts.

It was Bonnie's turn to fall under the man's regard. His green eyes gazed at her unblinking. "You are?" he prompted.

Automatically, Bonnie cast her eyes down and dipped a small curtsey. "Hodges, sir, the governess."

"Did the boys want to see me then? They heard their uncle had arrived?"

Bonnie was confused. "I was unaware they had any uncles."

He waved her off. "I will see them later. I am awaiting the viscount."

Henry drew a deep breath as though he were about to speak, but nothing came out.

Bonnie kept her voice steady and quiet. "Henry is the viscount, sir."

Mr. Montgomery furrowed his brow. "I know very well who the viscount is, Miss Hodges. I am friends with their father."

Now Henry had moved to stand against her skirts, although he didn't clutch her legs as Arthur did. "I regret to inform you that both the viscount and his wife recently perished in a coaching accident. Henry is the viscount."

His eyes narrowed. "Impossible."

"I assure you, I speak true."

He looked around, seeming to finally take note of the atmosphere of mourning. Rubbing his face, he stepped away, giving them his back. "When?"

"Two months ago."

"Bloody mail service," Bonnie thought she heard him mutter. He turned back to her. "Who is in charge?"

"Forgive my impertinence, sir, but I do not see how that is relevant to you."

His jaw set. "A governess has just informed me of the death of my friend. Relevance has little place in this situation. Answer the question."

Bonnie kept her gaze steady. "We are awaiting the guardian named in Viscount Darrow's will."

"And he has not arrived in two months' time?"

"Clearly not. Otherwise you would not have to lower

yourself to conversing with a governess." She couldn't keep the cutting tone from her voice.

A muscle in his cheek pulsed; otherwise his face remained impassive. "Who is the named guardian?" he asked in a cold voice. "My friendship with the viscount leaves me concerned for his children."

"I do not know," Bonnie confessed, her eyes on Arthur's head. "I was not present for the reading of the will and Mr. Renard has not seen fit to inform me."

The man took a deep breath. "Then bring Renard here."

"He is not here at present. Mr. Burdis might know," she offered. At the man's nod, Bonnie called the butler in. "Mr. Burdis, have you heard the name of the guardian?"

Burdis cleared his throat. "Indeed I have, Miss Hodges. Not necessarily by proper means, you understand."

Bonnie smiled. "You are too righteous for your own good. None here is a priest."

A smile pursed the butler's lips. The tall man left out a small sound of impatience. "Who is the guardian, Burdis?" he demanded.

Burdis blinked. "You are, sir. Viscount Darrow named Sir Stephen Montgomery as guardian to his children."

CHAPTER THREE

Stephen stood straight, his hands clasped behind his back as he regarded the recent graves of his friend and wife. Seeing the epitaphs compounded the reality—George Darrow, his friend for nearly twenty years, was dead, along with his wife Roslyn.

He swallowed against the tightness in his throat. "I am sorry, old friend," he said quietly. "I wish I had arrived earlier. But that cannot be changed. Be assured that I will assume my guardianship with all the gravity it warrants. Your sons will be a credit to your memories." With a deep breath, Stephen placed his hands on the tombstones. "I will miss you both."

Clearing his throat, Stephen left the cemetery and rode away from the town church, back to Darrowgate where a multitude of tasks awaited him, the first of which was to speak to that governess. "Burdis, send the governess to me."

"Yes my lord, but she is lunching in the nursery."

"Now, Burdis." He went into the study. There was no hesitation until he was actually sitting in his late friend's chair behind the desk. He knew it was impossible, but a small, fanciful side of him could still feel George's warmth in the leather.

Stephen had regained control of himself by the time the governess arrived, the boys a step behind her. He was silent until they were standing before the desk. "I did not say to bring the children."

"With respect, my lord, the children do not leave my presence."

"Your zealous protection does you credit, but they will be fine with a maid for a few minutes. Send for one."

"You misunderstand me, sir. It is the boys who do not leave me, not the other way around."

Stephen looked at her, his brow furrowed. "Ridiculous. They are children. Call a maid or footman."

He watched as the governess, trailed by the boys, went to the door and called for a footman. As they waited, Stephen considered how more biddable she was than earlier. Perhaps she was intelligent enough to realize that whatever position of power she had was no longer realistic.

Stephen stared in disbelief at the ruckus the children made when the footmen tried to lead them away. Henry cursed the servant as only an eight-year-old can, arms and legs flailing, while Arthur clung so viciously to the governess's legs that she was being dragged out the door, an unholy noise emanating from his mouth. Although the footman managed to carry Henry out of the study, the boy dashed back in immediately and grabbed the other side of the governess's legs, increasing his protesting volume.

"Enough," Stephen roared over the commotion. Everyone froze. "Your point is taken," he bit out.

"They will sit and be silent, sir." At her gentle push, the boys sat on a sofa on the other side of the study. "They will not disturb us unless necessary."

"What had brought on this ... attachment?" Stephen asked, glancing at the children.

The governess regarded him for a moment before lowering her eyes to the desktop. "They witnessed the death of their parents. I was there as well."

"And they are constantly with you ... my apologies; I cannot remember your name."

"Hodges, sir, and yes they are. Even if they wake at night and I am not in the same room, their panic is similar."

"I see." Stephen rubbed his forehead and changed the subject. "Why are there so few servants?"

"They began leaving several weeks ago once Mr. Renard made it clear no wages would be forthcoming until the guardian approves it."

"Who is Renard? This is the second time you have mentioned him."

"The late viscount's man of business."

"He has taken charge?"

"Until the guardian arrived."

"I will see to rectifying the situation. It appears there is much to be done."

Stephen watched as Hodges folded her hands in front of her. It was only for a moment; the smallness of her hands was distracting. Delicate and slender, they were used gently, deliberately. They brought to mind a field of heather stirred by the wind—a soft touch that belied an unexpected strength.

Stephen brought his gaze back to her face. "Why did you remain if wages were not being paid?"

Her eyes flicked to his momentarily. "The boys formed their attachment quickly. It seemed cruel to become another person who left them."

Stephen nodded. "Admirable of you."

Bonnie glanced over her shoulder at the boys before looking straight at him and lowering her voice. "The boys are suffering from severe trauma. They know me and I care for them. Henry and Arthur need someone they can trust. There is nothing admirable about it." Her tone was stern.

His eyebrows raised in surprise at this wisp of a governess chastising him. Clearly Hodges *had* been offended and wasn't afraid to make that known.

He cleared his throat. "My apologies, Hodges. I meant only that your sense of duty is admirable."

Henry interrupted, surprising them both. "It is Miss Hodges." His voice was a dry squeak, fighting his nerves.

Stephen gave the boy a quick glance. "My apologies, *Miss* Hodges," he amended.

She nodded, accepting his apology. "Is there anything else you wish to know?"

"No, that will be all for now."

Stephen waited until the door shut behind them before pulling a crinkled piece of paper from the inner pocket of his coat. Unfolding it, he smoothed it gently onto the blotter. He had read it several times before, but it held a new significance now. He scanned the contents until he came to the relevant part.

George had written:

There is something afoot here, Stephen, and I cannot put my finger on it. My worry increases daily, not for myself, but for my family. Small accidents are becoming larger and harder to explain away and no longer involve only me. You must come, I beg of you. You have always had a knack for ferreting things out. The safety and well-being of my family depends on it. There is no one I trust more.

The letter was dated only five days before his death; Stephen had not received it until two weeks after. Even with wrapping up his affairs as quickly as possible, it had still been two months before he arrived to help.

But he could not change the past. All Stephen could do was honor his friend's dying wishes—and find his murderer.

CHAPTER FOUR

Bonnie left the door open a discreet amount, allowing a shaft of light to penetrate the darkness of the chamber. The boys were finally asleep and she could escape for a short while, praying they wouldn't wake while she was gone.

It was the time of day she could call her own and a cup of tea in the warm kitchen beckoned. If she were fortunate, Mrs. Dabbs would even have left out a small plate of biscuits for her to enjoy.

Descending the staircase, she trailed her fingers along the bannister. Dreaming of that plate of biscuits, Bonnie did not notice a figure standing halfway to the landing until she reached the last flight. Stopping, she took in the tall stature of Sir Stephen, his hands folded behind his back; even from this distance, she could see the intensity of his gaze was directed at the portrait of the viscount and his wife.

Bonnie was uncertain about what to do. It was clear he was having a private moment. How could she get past him without disturbing him?

Biting her lip, Bonnie considered going to the closest servant's stairs. Yet they were back up half a flight and down two corridors. With the limited time she had, was that a realistic option?

"You are thinking very loudly, Miss Hodges."

A startled squeak escaped her. "Forgive me, sir. I had no intention of disturbing you."

Sir Stephen turned his head towards her. "I am merely looking at a portrait."

"There are people who dislike being distracted while studying them. They say it ruins the experience."

An eyebrow quirked. "You have met such people?"

Bonnie raised her eyes to his for a moment. "Some objected to such young boys being allowed in the National Gallery. We did not stay much longer after that."

A brief smile touched his lips and Sir Stephen looked back at the portrait. "A governess who sees the importance of an artistic education. How modern."

Bonnie bristled at his words. "Indeed, sir. Excuse me please." Taking care to not let her skirts touch him, she moved past him and continued towards the kitchen.

She had just finished pouring her cup of tea when Sir Stephen filled the doorway. They stared at each other for several long moments. Finally, without speaking, Bonnie took out another cup, poured some tea into it and sat down.

Sir Stephen took the seat across from her, pulled the extra cup of tea to him and added sugar. "I thought you could not leave the boys," he said.

Bonnie selected a biscuit from the plate. "I manage to have a few minutes to myself every evening once they finally are asleep. I try to get back before either of them have a chance to wake." She bit into her biscuit. She sighed with deep pleasure as the sweet treat filled her mouth.

Sir Stephen ignored the plate and set his tea down. "Tell me about the accident."

She brushed the crumbs from the corner of her mouth and took a fortifying sip of tea. "I would prefer not to."

"I need to know. It is important."

Bonnie looked at him. Strange, to be sitting here with someone who was her better. Sitting as equals in a half-lit kitchen, having tea. The look on his face was hard, but she did not feel threatened or intimidated. After seeing him on the stairs, she knew this was a man who wanted answers about his friend's death.

She took the last biscuit from the plate. Thankfully, Mrs. Dabbs knew not to put out more than two, if only for the sake of Bonnie's waistline. "It is not a pleasant tale," she said.

"I need to know," he reiterated.

Bonnie took a deep breath. "The boys and I had been cooling ourselves by the river. They always try to get me to swim with them, but I am content with dangling my feet off a rock. There is a place good for swimming, but the boys particularly like it because it is close the bridge and they can see the coaches crossing. When they see their parents' coach, a quick run over the hill allows them to arrive at the manor just as the coach is pulling up."

Bonnie continued, lost in the story and her memories. "The boys were swimming, watching for the coach. We couldn't see anything wrong from where we were; I'm still not entirely sure what happened. We saw the coach come around the bend. Henry was the first to recognize it; it's a contest between the boys. They began waving and calling out to get their parents' attention. Lady Darrow waved from the window as the coach began to cross the bridge.

"I heard a loud crack and the bridge started to shudder and give way. The coach was barely halfway over; there was nothing the coachman could do. I know it happened quickly, but in my mind it seemed to take forever, watching the bridge buckle, the coach following the splinters of wood down onto the rocky riverbed.

"The horses screamed. I remember that. They had to be shot. We weren't there for that. I don't know how long it took me to react, but I gathered the boys and hurried them back to the manor. Mr. Burdis must have sent some men from the Hall, but I don't know; I took the boys straight away to the nursery. Neither of them had spoken or made a sound."

Bonnie stopped speaking, staring blankly at the wall. Unconsciously, she lifted her cup to her lips and drained the last of her now tepid tea.

Stephen spoke. "Did they die immediately?"

She swallowed. "I heard that Viscount Darrow had broken his neck. Lady Darrow was not as fortunate. Apparently when the men found her, she was still breathing, but her stomach had been pierced by one of the wheel spokes. She did not last long after that."

Stephen sat back in his chair and absorbed the information. Bile rose in his throat at the thought of Roslyn dying in such a gruesome way. Mercifully, George's death sounded quick. It did not lessen the loss or shock, but it was a small blessing.

Gads, they were so young, he and George being of an age.

The thought of their lives being ended in such a way filled him with rage. Who could have done this? Who would have wanted this? George and Roslyn were not the kind of people to have enemies; they were too generous and caring.

Unable to contain himself, Stephen pushed his chair back abruptly and strode into the pantry. The door slammed shut behind him, but bounced open from the force of his thrust. Through the opening, Bonnie could see him approach the pile of flour sacks and attack it with a vengeance. She stared as he repeatedly punched them, splitting open the seams. He didn't make a sound, just continued to pummel the sacks, creating a light cloud around him.

After several minutes, Stephen's anger was spent. He stood staring at the pile of ruined flour, his body heaving from the exertion. Gaining control of himself, he smoothed his hair back and tugged on his waistcoat, straightening it. He took a deep breath and made his way back into the main kitchen, resuming his seat.

Bonnie stared at the man across from her. She could not reconcile the quiet, controlled man with the one she saw in the pantry. Indeed, if it wasn't for the thick layer of flour over his clothing and face, she would not believe they were the same man.

Stephen pushed his cup towards her. "I would like some more tea please."

A giggle of disbelief escaped her as Bonnie reached for the tea pot. Trying to suppress her amusement, she did as he bade, the teapot shaking from her effort. She could not hold the pot steady, instead spilling tea all over the table.

Bonnie put the teapot down and laid her forehead on the

table, shaking with laughter. Stephen looked at her in consternation, one eyebrow raised. "What is so amusing?"

His question made Bonnie laugh even harder, her arms clutching her middle. "You should see yourself," she hooted.

Stephen frowned. "What, pray tell, is wrong with my appearance?" He stood and grabbed a nearby pot to see his reflection.

The face staring back at him was covered in flour; his eyes appeared to be the only feature visible on his face. The same went for his hair. His attempt at smoothing it had only served to spread the flour more thoroughly on one side. Looking down at his clothing—what used to be black—Stephen could see that even the slightest movement created small puffs of flour clouds.

He looked back at Bonnie, still in the throes of her amusement. Tears were now streaming down her red face. A bubble grew in him. It could not be suppressed, but continued up and a sharp bark of laughter escaped him.

Bonnie's laughter was cut short at the sound. She stared at him, her chest heaving. What she saw on his face—at least what she could see of his face—triggered another fit of laughter. A deep chuckle came from him, joining in with the merriment. Soon, Stephen's laughter was uproarious. A part of him felt guilty at his behavior, but a larger part of him couldn't help but feel relieved.

Their laughter calmed to breathless giggles and chuckles. Stephen sat down again, his body relaxed and Bonnie wiped her face free of tears. After a moment of silence, Bonnie got up and retrieved a cloth to wipe up the spilled tea. "Neither of the boys slept for two days after the accident."

Stephen looked at her. Something about her face made him want to offer comfort, but for the life of him, he could not think of how.

With a final sigh, Bonnie gave him a curtsey. "I must return to the boys. Good evening, sir."

The return to formality triggered an automatic reaction in Stephen. He straightened in his chair and gave her a nod of dismissal. She was, after all, just a governess.

CHAPTER FIVE

Bonnie jerked upright into a sitting position, her chest heaving. Shreds of the nightmare still clung to her, the screams of horses and humans twisting in her mind, the sight of a collapsing bridge looming. Struggling to breathe, Bonnie untangled the covers from her legs and lurched up, heading for the window.

She pressed her forehead against the cool glass, using the cold reality to push back the nightmare. Slowly the image and sounds receded and her mind settled.

Moving away from the window, Bonnie turned and stood by the bed, watching the boys sleep. When it had become clear that they would not sleep alone or anywhere she was not, she moved them to the guest room with the largest bed and had a trundle bed brought in for herself. Once the boys calmed, they would return to their own chambers, but for now all were content with the arrangement.

With a weary sigh, she looked back at the small trundle bed. It held no allure for her; it offered no protection from the recurring nightmare. But dawn was still hours away and she could neither remain awake nor leave her charges for another room.

Without another thought, she eased herself over into the space between the two boys and pulled the cover over all three of them. Within moments, both had sought out her warmth and snuggled into her sides. Taking comfort from the weight of their small bodies, Bonnie drifted back into dreamless sleep.

Stephen grimaced against the bitterness of his second cup of coffee. He had not slept well the night before, jumping at every possible creak and groan the house made. Strange how different the place felt without George and Roslyn. Even the bed had felt less comfortable and the fire had lacked warmth. At least the food had not suffered. He gulped down the remains of the coffee and pushed away his empty plate. He had work to do.

He strode into the hall, calling for Burdis. "Have my horse saddled," he instructed the butler when he appeared.

"Sir," Burdis began.

"I'll be down momentarily," Stephen continued, making his way to the stairs. "I expect to be out for most of the morning."

"But—" Burdis tried again.

"I have little time to waste, Burdis," Stephen said.

"I couldn't agree more."

Stephen halted on the stairs. He turned to look at Burdis, not recognizing the new voice, but something tugged at his memory as he looked at the visitor. He stood in the drawing room doors, his hands behind his back and his eyes made owlish by a pair of spectacles. His gaze met Stephen's briefly before dropping respectfully into a bow.

Stephen studied the stranger as he made his way back down the stairs. He took in the man's stature, so tall and thin as to be likened to a flagpole. There were not many people Stephen had to tilt his head to look at, but this man clearly belonged in that category.

"Sir Stephen, it is a great relief to know you have arrived. Mr. Sylvester Renard at your service." The tall man straightened out of his bow.

The memory returned with that thought—George's man of business, Mr. Renard. Older than Stephen, Renard's dark hair had become liberally streaked with gray. His clothing struck Stephen as odd; while well-made and conservative, they were the exact brown of the walls, giving the impression of blending in. It seemed to take the idea of being an invisible servant to a new level. When Stephen did get a good look at the man of business, he thought a stiff Scottish wind would blow him over, he was so thin.

Stephen nodded his greeting. "I was unaware of the situation prior to my arrival yesterday. If I had known, I would not have delayed."

"Yes, of course." Renard adjusted his spectacles. "It was an unfortunate tragedy to lose Viscount and Viscountess Darrow in one fell swoop like that. I remain, however, at your service."

Stephen cocked his eyebrow. "Is any tragedy fortunate?" he queried.

Renard blinked. "Of course not, sir."

Stephen turned to the butler. "My horse, Burdis."

Renard interrupted. "If I may be so bold, the delay in your arrival has left a great deal that requires attention. Perhaps now is not a good time to leave?"

Stephen looked at the door. He had intended to ride over to where the old bridge had been, to examine it for any hint of anything suspicious. Time and inclement weather being factors, the probability of him discovering any such thing was already low; the thought of delaying even more did not sit well with him.

Yet Renard was also correct. Though he doubted an hour or two's delay would change the mountain of paperwork much, Stephen recognized the atmosphere clinging to the manor. It wasn't just mourning spoiling the mood, but resentment. As much as he wanted to discover more regarding his friends' deaths, he knew that George and Roslyn would want him to focus on caring for their sons. Doing so would honor their memories.

"Burdis, I will be going for a ride after luncheon. Be sure to have my horse readied then."

Stephen reined in his horse, Emperor, to study the river from a vantage point. A new stone bridge had been built a short distance upstream, but remnants of the destroyed wooden structure littered the riverbed. Around the area, trees had turned color and the grass had begun to wither; birds still flew through the air, not yet worried about the coming winter. Stephen had left his hat at home in light of the stiff October breeze and, feeling his ears and cheeks turning red, he momentarily regretted he had not worn a scarf.

Shifting in the saddle, he took in the surrounding land. Open fields hugged Darrowgate, copses of trees interspersed beatifically. Across the river, crops had been harvested; in other fields, cattle grazed. Beyond that, Stephen could clearly see the steeple of the town church and the thatched roofs of neighboring buildings.

Emperor tossed his head impatiently. Making a soothing cluck, he urged the horse into a walk down the hill towards the river. Coming up to the trees that lined the bank, Stephen dismounted and tethered Emperor in a spot where he could fill his greedy stomach with grass.

When he reached the water's edge, Stephen stopped. Staring at the wreckage that used to be the wooden bridge, he was acutely aware that he was staring at the site of his friends' deaths.

Images from the story Miss Hodges had told him flashed through his mind—the waving parents, the shuddering bridge before it collapsed, the falling planks and horses, the coach splintering, George's neck snapping and Roslyn—God, Roslyn lying in that mangled coach, her blood pouring out of her body. How had she survived long enough for anyone to come and see her still breathing?

Nausea roiled in his stomach and bile forced its way up his throat. Heaving, Stephen bent over a nearby bush and lost the contents of his stomach. Minutes later, he crouched down at the water's edge and splashed the cold water on his face.

From where he crouched, Stephen turned his gaze down the river away from ruined bridge. He could make out an area ideal for swimming; a small stretch of sandy bank surrounded by a few larger, flat rocks. Indeed, an excellent place for a governess to take her charges for a cooling swim on a hot summer day.

Stephen straightened and made his way along the bank to the swimming area. A well-worn path weaved through the bush, connecting the small beach to the hill beyond and Darrowgate. The bridge was 200 feet upstream; not only would the governess and the boys have a good view of the collapse, the blood from the incident would have flowed right by them.

No wonder they barely spoke.

Tearing his gaze from the bridge, he focused on the water, trying to imagine the trio enjoying their swim, with no inkling or threat of danger. The boys in the water, laughing and splashing each other, showing off their swimming skills to their laughing governess.

Stephen looked at the closest flat rock, the thought of the laughing governess in his mind. She had said she preferred dangling her feet instead of swimming.

His mind's eye put Miss Hodges on the rock, much as she had been the previous night. The look on her face after seeing his own flour-covered face. Her smile had been so wide it had been difficult to see anything else about her. He knew her eyes and hair were certain colors, but he was damned if he could name them—eyes were some light shade and the hair was brown, that he knew for certain.

And her laugh—it was the last thing he had expected from her. He was in a difficult situation—not quite master but regarded as such until Henry's majority. For a servant, even a governess, to laugh as she had was entirely unpredictable.

He shouldn't think too much about how that unexpected laughter had settled in his gut.

The image of Miss Hodges sitting on the rock rose again in his mind. The sun would have warmed the rock beneath her hands and she would have looked down at the clear water. She would laugh at the boys' antics, even kick water in their direction if they ventured too close. Her stockings would be folded into her shoes to keep them from blowing away in the breeze.

Good Lord, he could almost see it. The stockings protected in the nearby shoes, her naked feet dangling in the water, her skirts raised to keep them from getting wet, exposing her trim ankles. The clear water would do nothing to hide either her feet or her ankles and Stephen found himself staring unabashedly at something that wasn't even there. He stared at the empty water, imagining exactly what Miss Hodges' ankles would look like. They would be trim, they would be bonny, they would—

Thankfully, a passing cart made enough noise to break him out of this ridiculously schoolboy moment. Inhaling deeply through his nose, Stephen left the swimming area and made his way back for a closer look at the ruins.

Chapter Six

Dearest Claire,

I have to admit, I am not surprised that Mr. Knightly insisted so strongly on a short engagement. Did he actually show you the special license with the vicar standing right there? And over breakfast? I am gratified to know that you stood firm and insisted on waiting for morning lessons to be completed before any vows were spoken.

I do hope that wedded bliss and the happiness of the recently wed softens your reaction to what I am about to say. I know I promised to come to Ridgestone once the guardian arrived, but I must beg the Governess Club's patience. Sir Stephen Montgomery arrived eight days ago, yet I still do not feel the situation frees me to leave.

I know it is not my place to say so, but I am worried about his ability to be an adequate guardian to the children. Since his arrival, he has shown little to no interest in the boys, unless they find themselves standing before him, which is rare. Sir Stephen spends his time either in the study, mainly with Mr. Renard, or on his horse, riding the estate.

The only indications that the guardian has taken control of
the household is the increase of servants and the paying of
wages owed. I have already deposited my belated percentage
into the joint account.

Claire, he is so remote. Stern, silent, and awkward,
so unlike the guardian I expected Viscount Darrow to
appoint. Wouldn't he want someone more like himself? They
had been friends since school, but I cannot see it. I have
seen him laugh only once. On his first day here, he returned
from a ride with a piece of the ruined bridge; it remains in
the study. The following day he met with Mr. Burdis for
nearly two hours. When the butler left the study, he looked
as though he had withstood an interrogation at the Tower of
London.

Based on this, I cannot leave. I cannot leave Henry and
Arthur with a distant stranger. This goes beyond duty and
I am sure you can relate. I care for Henry and Arthur. And
I am all they have right now. I must remain. My conscience
and my affection demand it.

Please do not be angry with me. My intentions to
come to Ridgestone remain unaltered, just the timeline
in which I see myself joining you. I know Sara will
understand, but I am counting on your level head to keep
Louisa calm. She is bound to react poorly. Appeal to her
compassion; what woman would leave children in such a
situation?

I do expect this letter to reach you before you leave for
your wedding trip to Scotland, so I wish you a happy and
safe journey. Sir Stephen is from Scotland; did I mention
that? His brogue is not very thick, but it is there, so I suspect

he is from somewhere in the Lowlands. But I digress. If this letter happens to reach you after your trip, I hope you had a memorable time and either way, I look forward to hearing all about it.

    With all my love,
    Bonnie

CHAPTER SEVEN

Stephen leaned his elbows on the desk, rested his forehead against his fingers, and rubbed. He could not remember the last time his eyes and head ached in such synchronicity. For nine days, Renard had been pushing ledger after account after letter after bill under his eyes. Stephen considered himself a decently observant man, but even he could not determine any progress made on the piles of work in the study.

It all took away from what he actually wanted to do. Since Renard had gotten his claws into him, Stephen hadn't been able to investigate beyond the ruined bridge and interviewing Burdis. The butler had been surprisingly ill-informed regarding the accident; all he had been able to confirm was that George and Roslyn had seen an increase in their clumsiness in the months leading up to their deaths.

He looked at the standing clock. This was around the time the governess had gone to the kitchen last week. He had only seen her in passing since that night and had no idea if taking tea at this time was her routine. But if he did not at least try to look for her, who knew when his chance would be?

With that thought, Stephen stood and strode purposefully out the study. *It may be another nine days before I get this opportunity again. No sense letting it go to waste.*

The light filling the servant's corridor increased his certainty. He turned the corner and stepped into the kitchen light. Miss Hodges was sitting in the same chair as last time, her feet propped on the seat next to her, her head tilted back and eyes closed as she chewed. Stephen watched, mesmerized as any man would be, as Miss Hodges dramatically raised the last bit of biscuit over her head and intentionally lowered it to her open mouth.

"Mmm," Miss Hodges let out a moan around the biscuit. "Mrs. Dabbs, you do make a delicious biscuit. Absolutely sinful it is."

Stephen cleared his throat, alerting her to his presence. He didn't expect her shriek, or the flailing limbs rocking her off the chair and onto the floor. He winced at the sound of her body hitting the stone floor and moved around the table to assist her.

He found her on her hands and knees struggling to breathe. "Miss Hodges?" he asked. At her distressed hand signal, he quickly crouched down beside her and thumped her on the back. He did it again when she continued to struggle. And again. He raised his hand for a fourth time but she stalled him by sitting back on her heels.

Her face was red, her eyes watered, and her hair was disheveled from her ordeal. A few more coughs and she wiped her eyes and patted her hair.

"Are you all right?" Stephen asked.

Miss Hodges took a deep breath and pushed herself up

on shaky legs. Stephen automatically followed. "My lord," she said with an awkward curtsey. "Was there something you required?"

He was silent for only a moment. "Tea."

Miss Hodges gave a quick nod. "The water ought to still be warm. I will freshen the pot and bring you a tray in the study."

"Here is fine. You are not a kitchen maid."

She looked at him as she fetched another teacup. "No, but I am a governess, and governesses, my lord, have many talents. Besides, the kitchen maids get up early and accommodate me enough by leaving out the makings for tea."

Stephen sat in the same chair as he had last time. "Do you come here often?"

A small twinkle entered her eye. "To the kitchen? Usually whenever I am hungry."

He stared at her eyes. Green? No, hazel. That was their color. More of a green than brown, but definitely hazel.

The twinkle in those eyes faded when he did not respond. She dropped her gaze and gave a quiet "forgive me," and poured him his tea. Formality settled on her like a shawl where she stood.

He gestured at the tea service. "Please sit and finish your tea with me."

Bonnie sat hesitantly. She had been raised and trained for numerous situations she might experience as a governess, but never had taking tea with the master of the house in the kitchen been mentioned.

Sir Stephen took a sip of his tea and gestured to hers. "Finish your tea," he said quietly. Unable to do much else, Bonnie lifted the cup to her lips and took a sip. The warm liquid freed her throat of the lingering biscuit crumbs, much to her relief.

Sir Stephen spoke. "You misunderstood me earlier. I meant to ask if you take tea at this time regularly."

"Most evenings, yes, once the children have fallen asleep. Is it permissible?" She tried to keep the worry out of her eyes and voice. The viscountess had not minded, but this guardian was still unknown.

"Aye," he replied, inclining his head. "I have no intention of disrupting the household overly much."

Relieved, Bonnie looked into her tea. These moments alone in the kitchen had become a sort of sanctuary, even more so since the accident. She did not know what she would do if it were to be taken away.

"You don't believe me?" His voice cut into her thoughts.

"If I may be so bold, sir, this household had the largest disruption one could possibly fathom. The arrival of the guardian, while appreciated, hardly warrants panic."

"Are you suggesting that any changes I make would be received gladly?"

"I am saying that you are the master of the house. It is not our place to question whatever changes you make."

Stephen couldn't let that challenge pass. "So if I were to let you go, you would not object?"

Those hazel eyes revealed her shock again; she had quite expressive eyes. "Let me go?"

Stephen shrugged and took a drink of his tea. "Henry is of age to need a tutor and Arthur seems more in need of a nurse than a governess. On paper, it does not make sense to retain a governess at this point."

Bonnie couldn't speak. Was she truly being let go? While it would free her to go to Ridgestone Manor, the stain of having her employment terminated would attach itself to her professional reputation; the only acceptable time for a governess to be let go was when the last child graduated from the schoolroom. Besides, Henry and Arthur still needed her. They still had so much to recover from and taking away the one person they depended on would likely hinder that process even more.

And to leave them with this man who regretted his guardianship only nine days in? She could not do it; every part of her being screamed in denial. What would he do for the next thirteen years if he already wanted to forget his responsibilities?

"You would get a glowing recommendation, of course," he continued speaking. "Anyone with eyes can see the good you have done, especially given these strained circumstances."

"Thank you," Bonnie managed to say around the blockage in her throat.

"I am confident you would find another post. You are a governess and there are always families in need of one."

Oh, what a way to put her in her place. Of course she was just a governess. Her employment depended on the whim of those controlling the money and making the decisions.

Heaven help her, she had grown too secure with the thought that the boys needed her so desperately. She had forgotten everything her mother had taught her, everything her father had shown her. She had even ignored the warnings Louisa had given. This was the very reason why she wanted the Governess Club formed, to protect herself and the others from arbitrary decisions and mistreatment. How could she have been so stupid as to relax?

Bonnie cleared her throat and stood. "Would you prefer me to leave immediately or to remain until the tutor and nurse are found?"

Stephen raised his eyebrows. "You have no objections?"

"It is not my place to object, my lord."

He sat back and regarded her closely. She had said any changes would be accepted by the servants without objections, and here she was, standing in the face of dismissal with dignity and poise. It appeared she was a woman of her word, indicating she could be trusted.

"Sit down, Miss Hodges," he said. His voice was again quiet, but Bonnie felt the order in his words nonetheless and complied. "Tell me what I said."

Bonnie stared at him and said, "You said you were letting me go."

"Did I?"

Bonnie furrowed her brow and thought again. "You said there is no reason to keep me and so were letting me go."

"Not quite. Think hard."

Taking a deep breath, she thought about everything he said. Every word floated through her brain. When her mind honed in on a significant point, she blurted, "You said that it did not make sense on paper to retain me."

Triumph flared in his eyes. "Does that say beyond a shadow of a doubt that I will let you go?"

"No."

"Why not?"

"It indicates that there is more affecting your decisions than things you can see on paper."

The corners of his mouth tugged into a small smile. "Excellent. It is clear that the boys depend on you and that you have a calming effect on them. It would be a grave mistake to let you go."

Relief flooded through her body. Stephen could see it in the way her body sagged. As dignified as she had taken the thought of her dismissal, it had frightened her.

The relief lasted only a minute. Anger filled her hazel eyes. "Was this some sort of a test?"

"I suppose you could look at it that way."

"Is this what you do for amusement? Is this meant to make me appreciate you for not letting me go?"

"No. If it makes you feel better, you passed."

"And what would have happened if I had not?"

Stephen shook his head and answered, "I would not have trusted you."

Bonnie let out a disbelieving laugh. "Not trust me? What have I done since your arrival to indicate that I am not trustworthy?"

"Nothing comes to mind."

"Well, I certainly feel assured that the man who has done nothing to gain our trust feels that I am worthy. If you will excuse me." Bonnie pushed herself up and stormed around the table to the servant's corridor.

"Miss Hodges, I did not mean to upset you."

Bonnie turned and looked at Sir Stephen standing at the table. "The most important thing in my life at this moment is Henry and Arthur. It doesn't concern me that their new guardian apparently expects everyone to earn his trust before he takes any step to show himself worthy of the same regard."

"Miss Hodges, calm down."

"With respect, my lord," Bonnie continued. "What concerns me is that in the nine days since being here, their guardian has done nothing remotely guardian-like. And you think I am the one who needs to earn trust?"

Stephen stared at her. "Miss Hodges, I . . ."

"Do you understand, Sir Stephen? Do you understand that these boys need more than a man behind a desk balancing ledgers? They need more than someone who hires tutors and runs the estate. They need more than you; they need a father."

"I am not their father," Stephen burst out. "He is dead. My friends are dead. I am bloody well not some sort of savior."

"I know," Bonnie said, her voice sad. "But you're all they have."

CHAPTER EIGHT

"Enough." Stephen slammed his hand on the desk, cutting Renard's sentence off. "It's been ten days, Renard. Ten days of this."

"Sir—"

"No. I find it hard to believe that Darrow would let his estate get into such a mess."

"I understand, Sir Stephen. I assure you, I did my best, but in the last months, Lord Darrow was not himself."

Stephen's attention perked up at that. "Explain yourself."

Renard shifted uncomfortably. "I do not wish to speak ill of the late viscount."

"If you know anything that will help me through this," Stephen gestured at the piles of paper covering the desk, "then share it."

"Lord Darrow seemed ... distracted in the last few months," Renard offered.

"Elaborate."

"He did not spend as much time working with me as he had in the past. When he did come into the study, the decisions and investments he made—I may as well not have been in the room for how little he listened to me."

"Bad investments?"

"Yes sir. Not so much bad, but ill-advised. Companies and men seeking investors came. I advised against many of them, but he wouldn't listen."

"Why do you think that was?"

Renard shifted again. "He had been drinking, sir. Most of the time you couldn't find him without a glass in his hand."

Stephen's eyebrows raised. "Drinking?" Renard nodded. Stephen sat back in his chair, running his hand through his hair.

"The more he drank, the more suspicious he became," Renard continued.

"Suspicious?"

"Thinking someone was out to hurt him. His drinking had made him clumsy and he had several accidents. Once, I came into the study late at night and he was pacing, muttering to himself about someone targeting him and his family. But I never saw anything of the sort, nothing that couldn't be explained as drunken clumsiness."

Stephen rubbed the bridge of his nose. Could it be that the fear George had conveyed in his letter was the result of his own doing? It must have been written in a moment of sobriety; the lucidity indicated nothing else. Is it possible that he had been losing sleep over the actions of a sot?

"Renard," Stephen stood up. "I'll need to see all those bad investments. Find everything you can in all this."

"Yes sir."

Stephen ran the currycomb down Emperor's length. He did it again. And again. He relished in the shine of the gelding's chestnut coat, the smell of the stable; both had calming effects on him.

It didn't add up. Surely George would have known whether someone was actually targeting the Darrow family; it couldn't just be drunken illusions. Was the suspicion the result of drinking, or vice versa?

Stephen moved to Emperor's other side, trailing his palm over the horse's rump, and began brushing again. The repetitive routine, the normalness of the action, was soothing. Emperor was enjoying the attention; he kept turning his head towards Stephen, snuffling around for some sugar lumps or apples.

Stephen obliged Emperor, dipping into his pocket for the sugar lump. "Aye, I've been neglectful," he murmured with a smile. "We'll go for a run tomorrow, although it won't be much like what you are used to. No air from the firth here, no hills like those around Annan, but plenty of space to stretch our legs. Aye, even that river there is nice to look at, don't you think?"

"You talk to your horse?"

Stephen turned at the young voice to see Henry standing at the stable door with his brother and governess. Arthur, as he had come to expect, was holding Miss Hodge's hand and sucking his thumb.

Stephen focused on Henry. "Aye. Horses respond to sound and can identify human voices. Talking to your horse can build a bond between rider and mount. Besides, Emperor's a good listener."

Henry didn't smile, but he did take a step closer. "We've come to see the kittens. The barn cat birthed some last week."

"Indeed?" Stephen resumed brushing Emperor's back. "Cats are useful, but I prefer dogs myself."

"Why?"

Stephen shrugged. "I've always liked how dogs follow you around. You can walk for hours over the hills and they will stay with you. And you can always tell what they want, whether it is to chase after a bird or to chew on a bone. You can never tell what a cat is thinking."

"But cats take care of themselves, my lord," Miss Hodges joined the conversation. "Surely their independence speaks in their favor. A dog is nearly completely dependent upon its owner."

"All the more reason to trust its loyalty," he replied.

"But only until someone with a bigger bone comes along," she rejoined. "I find cats much more loyal than dogs; they are not so easily swayed by their physical desires."

Stephen stopped brushing for a moment, the thought of physical desires lodging in his brain. Surely she did not mean what he took her to mean. He cleared his throat and resumed brushing. When he didn't reply, Miss Hodges led the boys safely around the horses to the stall where presumably the cat resided.

"You brush your horse too?"

Stephen glanced over his shoulder and saw Henry standing outside the stall, watching him. "Aye. A good horseman takes care of his own mount."

"My father brushed his own horse. Not every day, but often."

"Come here," Stephen bade. When Henry came closer, he indicated how to come around Emperor safely. "Here," Stephen fished into his pocket for another lump of sugar. "Emperor has a sweet tooth. He won't bite you."

"I don't brush Emperor every day either," Stephen said. "A groom can do just as good a job as me and sometimes I am in a rush. But I like to do it when I can."

Henry had moved to stand beside Emperor's head and was stroking his neck. From the way the horse was blinking, Stephen thought he must be in some state of horse heaven.

"I have a Dartmoor pony," Henry said. "My father was teaching me to ride. He said I could have a stallion for my birthday."

Stephen doubted that very much. "We will have to judge your horsemanship first."

"But my father said—"

"Henry, did you know I met your father in school?" he interrupted. "We were in the same year at Harrow."

"I know he went there. I am to go there when I turn eleven."

"Aye. When you do, be sure to go to the stables. It was there your father and I spent most of our time."

"Why?" Henry was curious.

"Well, boys at that age aren't the sharpest. They like to let their fists do quite a bit of the talking. A boy with a Scottish accent and a boy who was smarter than even the older lads were easy targets. So your father and I spent most of our free time in the stables, learning about horses."

Stephen gave a faint, fond smile. "Grimsby was the stable master. The best thing he ever did for us was to treat us like we weren't special simply because we had titles before our names."

He looked down at Henry. The boy had his eyes on him, rapt. "Grimsby taught us that horses were to be respected. Part of respecting a horse is being aware of the danger it holds. An inexperienced or unsuspecting rider can put his life at risk the moment he mounts up."

"Truly?"

Stephen nodded and turned to face Henry. "Aye. And that is why I know your father did not promise you a stallion for your birthday. As much as he loved and respected horses, he loved you more and would not knowingly place you in a dangerous situation."

Henry turned red and looked down at the stable floor. "I am sorry for lying," he muttered.

"Henry, an intelligent man doesn't hide from mistakes, but learns from them. Do not lie to me again."

"Yes sir." Henry was still staring at the floor. "May I go now?"

"Aye," Stephen said. "The day after tomorrow I will watch you ride. I will see what your father has taught you and we can continue your lessons."

One corner of Henry's mouth lifted in a smile. "Truly?" At Stephen's nod, his eyes glowed. "Thank you sir. I look forward to it." He disappeared into the stall.

Stephen resumed brushing.

CHAPTER NINE

Gold mines in Cornwall. Corn fields in Scotland. Shipping lines to penal colonies in Australia. Expeditions to discover new rapid land-transportation lines to the East Indies. Investments swam before Stephen's eyes. What in God's name had George been thinking? Although according to Renard, George's mind had become too pickled to exercise sound judgment.

It was frustrating. Sickening even, sifting through the mess that was the last months of his friend's life. And all Stephen could think of doing next was shifting his attention to George's more personal correspondence to search for any clues.

How could he unravel this mess? The money spent on poor investments was gone; there was nothing he could do about that. He would have to be vigilant with future financial endeavors in order to recoup the losses. But hell, George had been the one with the head for numbers, not him. That made this whole situation even more bizarre to him.

"Sir, have you been to Astley's?"

Stephen's attention was jerked away from his depressive ruminations. "What was that, Henry?"

"Astley's Circus sir, in London. Have you been? I think it would be swell." Henry's face glowed with excitement from the top of his pony. The crisp late October air gave his cheeks a healthy red glow. "I would love to see the tricks they do on the horses."

"No, I haven't been," Stephen said, adjusting his grip on Emperor's reins.

"Perhaps we could go together to London? I think Miss Hodges and Arthur would enjoy it as well."

"I don't go to London often," Stephen said, his mind drifting back to the poor investments.

"Oh." The hope died in Henry's voice. "I don't think Miss Hodges is fond of horses anyway, but she likes fairs and fetes. I don't know if she has ever seen a circus. I haven't," he concluded quietly.

Stephen inhaled through his nose. "Why do you think she does not enjoy horses?"

Henry shrugged. "I have never seen her one on."

"Is that so?" There was a letter on George's desk asking for investors to fund a railway for transporting coal from Durham to the port in Stockton-on-Tees. "I don't understand it, sir," Henry continued. "How can a girl not like horses? Or frogs. I tried to give Elizabeth Talbot my pet frog and all she did was scream and run away."

Stephen gave a small smile. "Henry, the first thing you need to know about women is that they are not men." London was the highest consumer of coal in the British Empire; an efficient transport system could get coal to the city more quickly, yielding high profits.

"What does that mean?"

"It means that men will be men and ladies will be ladies. They like different things than us and we will never understand the appeal of the things they like." Investing in the railway as well as the coal mines it services could be a wise decision.

"And they don't like frogs or horses?"

"They like flowers and ribbons and teas and dances and pretty words. Men like horses and frogs and boxing mills and Scotch. We give ladies the flowers, ribbons, and pretty words because that's the only way we can get them to like us." The project had received parliamentary approval recently, making it even more viable. Renard should look into it.

"But Archibald was a magnificent frog. A prime jumper."

"Of course he was. But Miss Talbot saw a slimy thing that likes to eat insects." Stephen would write to his own advisor in Edinburgh. The man had proven to be thoroughly competent since he'd let his father's man go.

"Oh. So you are going to give Miss Hodges flowers and pretty words?"

That got his attention. "Excuse me?"

"Well, if you wanted Miss Hodges to like you, you could give her flowers and ribbons and pretty words."

Stephen reined to a stop and looked at Henry. "And what makes you think I want her to like me?"

Henry had a bit more difficulty pulling to a stop, but managed it. He didn't look at Stephen. "You are unmarried and my mother said that all unmarried men needed wives. My father would fight with her about it whenever one of his un-married friends would visit."

Stephen was amused. "And you think to continue her matchmaking ways?"

Henry hesitated. "I do not want her to leave, but I am too young to marry her myself."

Now it was Stephen's turn to hesitate. "Is she planning on leaving?" he asked carefully.

Henry visibly swallowed. "Many have. I do not want her to."

Hm. That made his stomach feel ... strange. "As my guardian," Henry continued, "you will be at Darrowgate until I come of age. If you married Miss Hodges, she would be here as well."

Stephen cleared his throat. "Your logic is flawless."

"Does that mean you agree? You will marry her for me?"

The boy sounded so eager. "No."

"But you said—"

"That your logic is flawless. I know," Stephen said. "Un-fortunately, you cannot apply logic to marriage."

"What do you mean?"

"Marriages based on logic and politics create unhappy people. Unhappy people are not beneficial to society; they have the potential to cause problems and destruction. If I were to marry Miss Hodges for your logical reasons, the po-tential for problems and destruction would be great."

"I don't understand, sir."

Stephen sighed. "Men are men and ladies are ladies, Henry. Men think with their minds, ladies with their hearts; they inevitably bring emotion into it, which never fails to muddy the waters. A logical marriage will only hurt a lady, which is something a gentleman should always try to avoid."

"Why?"

"Ladies have the uncanny ability to make things very unpleasant for us men."

"How?"

Stephen gave a sardonic smile. "I will tell you when you are older. Time to return to the manor." He waited until Henry was several feet in front of him before clicking his tongue, urging Emperor into a slow walk.

Marry Miss Hodges? Ridiculous. Stephen trailed Henry, allowing the boy to get a fair bit ahead of him. *Marry Miss Hodges? Preposterous.*

What advantages would there be to marrying the woman? Aside from a steady source of physical satisfaction, there were no reasons to take such a drastic step; his lustful fantasies of her would cease in time. Easing an eight-year-old's fear of abandonment was not incentive enough.

No. He was not going to marry Miss Hodges. He had barely finished cleaning up the mess his father had made and now he had to focus on cleaning up George's. He would not subject any potential wife of his to what his mother suffered her entire married life.

No, he would marry when he was a stable, financially viable prospect and not a moment sooner. He would enjoy his nighttime fantasies of the woman and continue to determine the color of her hair, but it would go no further than that.

Miss Hodges would not leave Darrowgate and he would not marry her. Everything would be fine. Stephen took a deep breath, loosening the tightness in his chest. He focused on

Henry, many yards ahead, already cresting the hill separating them from Darrowgate Hall. He squinted his eyes—was there something wrong with the girth on Henry's saddle?

Henry looked back at him with a wide grin. "They're waiting for us, sir! Let's race to them."

"Henry, no, wait," Stephen called out, but it was too late. Henry had already spurred his pony Harold into a quick canter. Stephen quickly did the same, not trusting Henry's skill in controlling the animal; the pony was not a large one, but it could still inflict damage.

Emperor's hooves pounded over the ground, carrying him quickly up to the top of the hill. Henry was still a good distance away, Miss Hodges and Arthur waving at his approach. The others were too distant to see the girth trailing on the ground underneath Harold and most definitely too far away to do anything about it.

Stephen's throat closed up, forcing him to deal with the blockage before being able to shout, "Henry, stop!" It came out hoarsely at first, so he repeated it with more strength.

Henry must not have heard him, for he continued with his pace. Stephen spurred Emperor into a full gallop, hoping to get to his ward before anything happened.

His hope went unfulfilled. Before his eyes, Stephen saw the saddle shift slightly to the side. Henry seemed to have noticed. His back stiffened, his entire body actually, and Stephen knew the boy had become paralyzed with the knowledge that something that wasn't right.

Shouting again, Stephen urged Emperor into a flat out gallop. He was getting closer by the second and braced himself to lift the boy from the pony. He gripped the reins in one hand and began to lean to the side he would approach Henry on. He flexed his fingers, not wanting to chance missing him.

The yards between them were shrinking. Stephen kept his eyes on Henry, willing the saddle to not slip any further.

Yet another hope unfulfilled; he would have to have words with the Higher Being in Charge. They would need to come to some sort of agreement if this guardian thing was going to work out well.

Chapter Ten

"Come now Arthur, what letter does fence begin with? Fuh-fuh-fuh-fence." Bonnie and Arthur were standing at the paddock fence, waiting for Sir Stephen and Henry to return from their ride. Arthur was hitting one of the rails, looking up at her. He wasn't smiling with his mouth, but Bonnie was sure there was a smile in his eye. "What about rail, sweetheart? Rah-rah-rah-rail. You have done this before."

Noticing some movement, Bonnie straightened and pointed, "Look, there's Henry." She lifted him to stand on the second rail, giving him a better view. "They're coming home from their ride. Let's wave them in." She held Arthur securely with one arm and waved with the other.

They watched and waved as Henry came galloping down the hill. Bonnie had a moment of fear that he was going too fast, that he wouldn't be able to handle the pony at that speed, but suppressed it, knowing that Sir Stephen likely had him practice out on the fields.

They watched and waved as they saw Sir Stephen crest the hill at a breakneck speed. Arthur kept waving, but Bonnie stopped as she saw Sir Stephen head directly for Henry. She heard his shout carried on the wind, couldn't make out the words but could clearly hear the panic.

Something was wrong. Desperately wrong. Sir Stephen wasn't a man prone to panic.

Arthur watched and waved. Bonnie watched, her heart moving into her throat, everything happening slowly as Henry slid to the side with his saddle. Sir Stephen was gaining on him, his arm outstretched to lift him from the pony to safety, but he was still so far away. At the last moment, Henry tried to grab at the pony's mane but missed and fell to the ground, the saddle bouncing over him.

Bonnie gasped as Henry tumbled over the ground, his body twisting and crumpling. Sir Stephen sawed on his reins, his horse heading straight for his now inert body. The horse reared at the sudden yanking of the reins and Bonnie felt a second type of fear at the prospect of the guardian being thrown from his horse. But Sir Stephen kept his seat, controlling his horse.

Without a thought, Bonnie placed Arthur on the ground, lifted her skirts and ran towards Henry, her thoughts already moving into dangerous territory. Behind her, she heard the shouts of several grooms and Arthur's shrieking. No choice but to ignore that; Henry needed her now.

Sir Stephen had already dismounted and was beside him by the time Bonnie reached him. She dropped to her knees and cupped Henry's face in her hands. "Henry, sweetie, wake up, wake up."

"He's out cold," Sir Stephen said. "Best move him now when he can't feel a thing."

"Henry," Bonnie repeatedly gave him light slaps in an effort to rouse him. "Wake up Henry. You're fine, you're not hurt."

Sir Stephen pushed her aside and scooped Henry into his arms. "Miss Hodges, see to Arthur. You there." He nodded to two grooms. "Fetch Emperor and Harold. You, go for the closest doctor. You"—he indicated a footman who had heard the commotion—"get Lord Darrow's saddle and bring it to the study. Lock it in there and don't let anyone in, not even Renard." He strode towards the house, not waiting to see if any actually followed his orders.

Bonnie hurried after him. "Henry is fine, is he not? He's not dead, he can't be dead. He's not hurt at all, is he? What will we do if he is hurt or dead?" She knew she was babbling but could not stop herself.

Sir Stephen halted. "Control yourself, Miss Hodges," he snapped, his brown eyes flashing. "You cannot indulge yourself. You need to see to Arthur. I will see to Henry for now. Arthur needs you. Remember that."

Bonnie drew in a shuddering breath. "You're right," she said, her head jerking in nods. "Arthur needs me. I will see to Arthur. We will look after Henry together. He must not see me panic."

Taking another deep breath to calm herself, she resumed walking, picking up the wailing Arthur when she reached him. "Let's go to the nursery, shall we sweetie?"

Bonnie knocked on the door to the viscount's study. At the gruff response, she opened the door and entered. It was late, yet the house had not yet settled for the night. The fright of losing a second viscount in as many months had shaken the very beams of the manor.

She stood unobtrusively just inside the room. Sir Stephen gave her a quick glance and stood. "Thank you, doctor," he said to the other man rising. They shook hands. "I appreciate your haste in coming here today."

"Quite right of me to do so," said the elderly man. "He is a boy, a viscount at that. Can't let another one go." He sighed deeply.

Sir Stephen closed the door after the doctor and moved back to the desk. "He says Henry will be fine. He has a dislocated shoulder and a small concussion. He has been given laudanum."

"Yes, I spent the last few minutes with him." Bonnie moved to stand in front of the desk. "Arthur would not settle until he saw his brother. We are much relieved to know that he is not seriously injured."

He cleared his throat. "It could have been worse."

"Yes. He was fortunate that he only fell from a pony and not that stallion he asked for three days ago." Bonnie smiled, but wiped it away when he gave her a look worthy of a basilisk.

This Sir Stephen behind the desk was much different than the one that took tea in the kitchen with her. Bonnie would do well to remember that. She had allowed herself to be drawn in by the casualness and intimacy of the kitchen, allowing herself to enjoy the Scottish lilt of his voice instead of remembering that he was the guardian and she was, quite simply, the governess. She had no business enjoying said lilt of his voice, nor thinking the memory of him racing to save Henry was reminiscent of medieval knights of old.

And that was that.

Sir Stephen handed her a list. He sat down and began to write on another piece of paper. When he didn't speak, Bonnie began to read it.

Her eyebrows rose before she even finished reading it. She cleared her throat.

"Is something wrong?"

Aside from your penmanship? "I don't understand what this is."

He didn't look up. "It is a list."

Well. "I do understand that much, sir. What I do not understand is the purpose for this list."

"You are to adhere to the restrictions detailed on that list."

She quoted, "All excursions from the manor are subject to your prior approval."

"Aye."

"I am to provide detailed itineraries of each approved excursion."

"Aye."

"If you are not available, I am to take two footmen or grooms as escorts."

"I am aware of what the list says."

"All encounters, however seemingly insignificant, are to be reported to you upon our return."

Sir Stephen sighed and tossed down his pen. "You have an issue with the list."

Smart man. "It is not my place to take issue, sir."

"And yet there you stand, taking issue." His tone was sardonic.

"Why the need for these restrictions?"

"I do not need to explain my reasons to you."

"Respectfully sir, my role is to provide superior education to Henry and Arthur. I cannot do so with these restrictions in place."

"You will have to adapt."

"I cannot."

"You must."

He brought to mind the moments when Arthur was at his most stubborn. "These restrictions are . . . restrictive."

Sir Stephen cocked a brow. "Was this an example of your ability to provide superior education?"

"What I mean sir, is that these restrictions will inhibit my ability to provide said superior education."

"Lord Darrow and I used to see how many times we could get our professors to speak a certain phrase during a lecture. Shall we see how many times we can say *superior education?*"

Bonnie took a breath to control herself. "Sir, you are making light of what I think to be a serious matter."

"Actually, what I am trying to do is distract you. It does not appear to be working."

"Please explain to me the need for these restrictions."

"No."

"Sir, I must insist—"

"Miss Hodges, you have a rather arbitrary definition of what your position as governess allows you to do."

"Respectfully sir, as I said, my priority is the education

of Henry and Arthur. Recently this has expanded to include their safety and well-being."

"You adapted."

"Yes."

"Adapt again."

"The reason for my adapting was clear, sir, something that is lacking in this situation."

Stephen sighed. She was not going to let this rest. "Can you not simply accept that I am acting in the best interests of the boys?"

"Not when you wish to inhibit the performance of my duties to such an extent."

He leaned back in George's chair. Had Henry seriously thought they would have rubbed on well enough to make a marriage work? The woman was impossibly stubborn. Intelligent, yet stubborn.

Stephen regarded Miss Hodges, standing before him, the desk between them. She was wearing a plain, modest green gown, her hands folded in front of her and the demure expression on her face, eyes connected with his, belied the persistence she was currently demonstrating.

He almost felt pity for Henry and Arthur.

His eyes focused on her hands again, much as they had on his first day as guardian, in the same position they were in now. Again he was struck by the smallness, the delicacy of her fingers. Again, despite that, he could sense the strength in them, the confidence in them.

From her hands, it was only a moment away from her wrist and up her nicely curved arm, to the hollow of her collarbone and neck, down to the nice swell of her bosom and back up until his eyes once again rested on her face. Her slender delicacy hid strength, certainty, and capability, unlike his own mother.

It didn't hurt that he liked the way she looked as well, this Miss Hodges with her hazel-green eyes, her appealing breasts, and her bonny ankles that haunted his dreams, even though he hadn't seen them yet.

Stephen refocused his eyes to find that hers had not wavered from his and now held a hint of censure. He cleared his throat and sat up, feeling his neck warm underneath his collar. Based on her position with the boys, he could see the advantages in confiding in her. If the boys were at risk, then she should be made aware of this. Her proximity to her charges placed her at risk as well and that thought made his skin prickle.

But first, he had to indulge himself for a moment. "Miss Hodges, what is your name?"

She blinked at the change in subject. "My name?"

"Your Christian name."

"Bonnie, sir."

Bonnie. Bonnie with the bonny ankles. A bonny lass. How fitting. He allowed himself a small smile.

"Miss Hodges, these restrictions are necessary after what happened to Henry today."

"He had an accident," she replied. "As young boys are prone to do. There is little reason to prohibit their movements to such a degree."

"I disagree—".

"Sir, these restrictions are reminiscent of Newgate or Bedlam, not a home."

"Miss Hodges, is interruption one of the skills you teach in your superior education?"

She took a breath and bowed her head briefly. "I apologize, sir."

He nodded in acknowledgment. "This was not an accident. There is a threat to Henry's life, possibly Arthur's as well."

"With respect sir, he fell off his pony. Many young riders do so."

"He didn't fall."

"I was there. You were there. He fell."

Stephen stood up and moved around the desk. "No he didn't." He strode to the sofas in front of the fire. Behind one, he produced Henry's saddle and placed it on the sofa. "What do you know about saddles?"

"Not much. I am not a rider."

"Come here," he gestured. Stephen knelt down and fingered the girth. "The girth goes underneath the horse's belly to secure the saddle. Henry fell off the horse because the girth was no longer holding it in place."

"He didn't secure it properly?"

Stephen held up the buckle. "I checked it myself before he mounted. The buckle is intact." He slid his hand to the broken section. "The girth snapped."

He held the broken girth to show her. Miss Hodges looked at him questioningly before kneeling down beside him and taking the girth from his hands. Her fingers brushed his palm momentarily, sending tingles up his arm. He cleared his throat again. "What do you notice about this?"

She fingered the tear. "Why is it only partially frayed?"

Sir Stephen ran a hand through his hair. "It had help.

Someone cut it in a discreet spot underneath the flap and to an extent that a ride, especially ending with a gallop, was enough strain to complete the damage."

Bonnie was dumbstruck. Her eyes were wide when she lifted them to the man kneeling next to her. "Wha—"

Sir Stephen stood and retrieved something else from behind the sofa. He placed a large plank of wood across the saddle and knelt down again. He pointed at one end and Bonnie turned her eyes there.

Similar to the girth, part of the end was splintered, but a good two thirds of it was a smooth angled cut, such as made by a saw.

Dear heavens. "From the bridge?" she choked out.

"It was only a matter of time before it gave out. There is no telling who would have been crossing at the time."

"So it—I—when . . ."

"Yes, it could have been you on the bridge."

Bonnie took in a shuddering breath. It didn't reach her lungs, so she tried again. And again.

She pressed a hand to her stomach. "I can't breathe."

Sir Stephen moved quickly, his fingers undoing the laces at her back. Once accomplished, he went to the decanter table and poured two generous glasses of Scotch. Bringing them over to her, he held one out.

"No, breathe, I need to breathe." She was gasping deeply.

"This will help you." He forced the glass to her mouth and poured a bit down her throat. She choked and sputtered and he did it again. The fiery liquid trailed down her throat, drawing tears to her eyes and burning her stomach. Bonnie gasped, air finally making its way to her lungs.

"Better?"

She nodded. "What do we do?"

His voice was solemn. "We must keep this quiet. I believe the attacks may be on the viscount title itself, so if Henry comes to harm, attention would shift to Arthur."

"But they are children!"

"I highly doubt that matters. And as their governess, you are likely to be caught in the line of fire."

Bonnie swallowed, her throat working tightly. "My mother raised me to be a governess. Prepared me for a wide range of situations. This was not one of them." She took a sip of the remaining Scotch. She turned to look at him. "How did you know?"

Stephen didn't pretend to misunderstand her. He pulled out the much-creased letter he always carried in his coat's inner pocket. "Darrow wrote me less than a week before his death. I didn't receive it until two weeks after. Read this paragraph." He pointed.

Bonnie scanned the contents and then had to read it again. "So when Lady Darrow—"

Stephen stopped her there. "Don't. Do not start analyzing every incident. There is no way to tell what was intentional or not. I was extremely lucky with the bridge."

Bonnie looked down at the letter again. "And he asked for your help?"

"Yes. We knew each other for nearly twenty years."

"Yet I hadn't met you before two weeks ago."

He shifted uncomfortably but remained silent. After a moment, he stood and offered her his hand. Bonnie took it, noting the calluses and the warmth. When she stood, her loosened gown gaped open and she had to clutch it from falling off.

Stephen stared. He couldn't help it. If he was any sort of gentleman, he would divert his eyes and give her a chance to right herself. But he couldn't stop staring. Her gown had shifted enough to reveal the swell of her bosom and edge of her cotton shift.

Dear God, and he had thought fantasizing about her ankles was provocative. Now he had an image of her exposed breasts that would linger when he closed his eyes at night. The creamy mounds glowed in the candlelight and he thought he could see the edge of dusk-colored areolas. Sweet Mary and Joseph, the urge to press his face in her cleavage rose up with a near violent need, to learn the scent of her, to taste her breasts and pillow his head on them as he slept.

"Could you retie my laces, please?"

Her soft voice jerked Stephen back to attention. In his distraction, Miss Hodges had turned her back to him and was waiting patiently for him to fix what he had undone. He swallowed against the tightness in his throat and reached for her laces; he had to flex his fingers to stop trembling.

"Who else knows about this?" Miss Hodges asked when she was able to face him again.

Stephen moved to the door but did not open it. He forced his eyes to stay on her face. "No one."

Her brows raised. "No one? Not Mr. Renard?"

"No. Darrow said he did not know who to trust. I see no reason to trust a man I do not know."

She paused in front of him, completely unaware of his

struggle to keep his eyes above her chin. "Yet, you trust me," she said softly. "Should I be honored?"

He tilted his head and placed his hand on the doorknob. "You have proven yourself."

A faint blush covered her cheeks and she smiled to his chest. Stephen opened the door for her. "Thank you," she said. "Good night." She dropped a curtsey and was gone, leaving Stephen alone with visions in his head and a lingering scent of sweetness in the air.

CHAPTER ELEVEN

Several days later, Bonnie and Arthur entered the house in a fit of giggles from the race they were having. "Oh no, you don't," Bonnie cried, scooping up the boy. "You're not going to win. I will get to the stairs first."

Arthur shrieked and struggled in her arms until Bonnie pretended to drop him, giving him the lead again. She followed in a flurry of skirts and gasps, their rapid footsteps resounding in the manor's large foyer. A footman caught off guard had to scamper out of the way; Burdis gracefully raised the tray of glasses over their heads and continued on as though nothing out of the ordinary happened.

Arthur reached the stairs by one stride ahead of Bonnie. She picked him up again and collapsed on the stairs, tickling him until he was gasping for breath. "How dare you beat me?" Bonnie teased, her fingers eliciting more giggles from him. "Don't you know you're supposed to let ladies win, you silly boy!"

Arthur sat up, wrapped his arms around her neck, and planted a sloppy kiss on her cheek. He pulled away and gave her a broad grin. Bonnie smiled back at him. "Oh you, sir, are going to be a charmer when you grow up, aren't you?"

"Miss Hodges, do you need some help?"

"Hm?" Bonnie glanced up to see Alfred, a footman who had been at Darrowgate for several years. "Excuse me?"

"Do you need help?" Alfred repeated. "With Master Arthur, miss. I can take him upstairs while you put yourself to rights."

Alfred. A good footman, efficient and solicitous. A quiet man. Silent to the point of reticence. He had been working with her for four years and Bonnie couldn't even say if he was originally from the area.

Send Arthur with him? Absolutely not.

Bonnie smiled and got to her feet, ensuring Arthur did the same. "No thank you, Alfred. We are fine. Do you know if Mrs. Dabbs sent up tea to the nursery yet?"

"I believe so, miss."

"Excellent." Bonnie took Arthur's hand. "Let's head up there and sneak a bit before Henry and Sir Stephen come, shall we Arthur?" He shared a conspiratorial smile with her and followed Bonnie up the stairs.

Good heavens, she hoped Sir Stephen would clean up this mess quickly. It was exhausting being so suspicious of everyone. All the time. Exhausting. Yes, it needed repeating, even in the privacy of her mind.

"Are you hungry?" she asked Arthur as she helped him take off his coat and hat. The late October day, even with the sun shining as it was, still had called for warmer clothes. She took her own cloak off and hung it up in the nursery closet. Arthur made a dash for the tea tray. "Oh no, young man, stop right there."

Arthur stopped and looked at her.

Bonnie arched her brows. "Are you supposed to leave your coat and hat on the floor?"

With a dramatic sigh, Arthur turned back and stomped slowly to where he had dropped them. Bonnie nodded with approval and made her way to the tea tray. "Mmm, biscuits."

Stephen watched as Henry once again correctly put a saddle on Harold. "Excellent work, Henry."

"Thank you sir. I won't mistake it again."

Stephen smiled. "Start taking it off now," he instructed. "Don't make the mistake of thinking you will never fall again. Accidents happen. They can make you a better rider, if you choose to learn from them." He moved to lift the saddle off of Harold; Henry's shoulder was still too pained to do heavy lifting.

"I believe Miss Hodges will be holding tea for us," Stephen said.

Henry smiled. "You don't know her very well. If Mrs. Dabbs has put biscuits on the tray, it would take an armed guard to keep her from them."

"Then let's go keep her from eating them all."

They entered the manor and left their coats with Alfred. They were halfway up the main stairs when an unholy wailing reverberated through the walls, halting them in their steps.

"That's Arthur," Henry said, worry in his face and voice.

Stephen sprinted up the stairs, leaving Henry to follow. What could have happened? And where was Miss Hodges and why wasn't she quieting Arthur?

Stephen burst through the open nursery door. He immediately saw the tea tray set up on the table, but what caught his attention was Miss Hodges on the floor, clutching her middle and moaning, tears flowing down her face. Arthur sat beside her, continuing his horrible howl, his face wet.

There was a half-eaten biscuit on the floor beside her.

Stephen didn't hesitate. He knelt down beside her. "Miss Hodges," he said over the noise. "Miss Hodges!"

"It hurts so much," she moaned.

"Where?"

"My stomach."

"Right, you're not going to like me for this. Henry, get the chamber pot." The boy rushed to do so and Stephen pulled her onto her knees, supporting her around the waist. With his free hand, he forced open her mouth and stuck his fingers in to the back of her throat.

She choked and gagged; Stephen felt it around his fingers. When her throat convulsed, he bent her over so she could be sick into the pot. Arthur howled even louder.

Stephen repeated the process.

Henry looked sick himself. "Disgusting!" he exclaimed.

Stephen shot him a look. "Take care of Arthur. Quiet him."

"Yes sir. Is she going to be sick again?"

"No, please," she begged.

"We must." He put action to words and held her as once more she emptied the contents of her stomach..

"Enough," she pleaded. "There's nothing left."

"That's the point," he replied. He supported her as Miss Hodges slumped against him, drained of energy.

Miss Hodges weakly raised her head and looked at him.

Her bonny hazel eyes were a mixture of pain and misery. It tore his insides. "The boys . . ." she whispered.

"Are fine," he replied.

Relief momentarily dispelled the pain and misery before her eyelids fluttered. Her eyes rolled back into her head and her head slumped against his shoulder as she fell unconscious.

Stephen held her close and eyed the biscuit on the floor. He glanced back at the door where several maids and footmen stood watching. "Clean this up," he instructed the servants. While they were distracted with following his orders, he scooped up the biscuit from the floor and snatched two more from the plate and pocketed them.

He stood, taking Miss Hodges with him and lifted her into his arms. He strode out of the nursery, holding her limp body close.

Chapter Twelve

She had regained consciousness briefly but was sleeping now. The doctor had said she was going to be fine. He had wanted to bleed the poison from her, but Stephen had been adamant, so the compromise was laudanum to help her sleep.

Stephen squinted against the sun reflecting off the lake. A few ducks remained, having grown fat and used to being fed by the members of the household. He tossed some more crumbs onto the water, waiting for them to stop resisting temptation.

Henry and Arthur were with her, once again refusing to leave her side. Newly hired servants were whispering of leaving, according to Renard. The air of distrust was growing, the more superstitious muttering of curses.

Stephen had interrogated Mrs. Dabbs. Renard had been in the kitchen when he arrived, holding the middle-aged woman as she cried, kissing her on the forehead in unmistakable intimate comfort.

Renard had refused to leave. "We were keeping it quiet, sir," he said. "I see no point in doing so now. Mrs. Dabbs and

I have been stepping out for some months now. We intend to marry."

"I will save my good wishes for a more appropriate time," Stephen replied.

"Sylvester—Mr. Renard was with me while I was making the biscuits." Her eyes swam with tears. "I swear I didn't do anything to them. I baked them just as the masters like. I would never harm them."

Renard had confirmed that. "I didn't see her or anyone put anything unusual in the biscuits."

Stephen threw more crumbs on the water, the ducks losing their initial shyness and enjoying the food.

Questioning the maid who carried the tray had resulted in nothing as well. All Stephen had was another crying female on his hands and no information.

Stephen watched the ducks eat. One began to cough, followed by the others. Some tried to fly, to escape what they sensed as danger, but could not get off the water. Sounds he had never heard before came from their convulsing bodies. The whole process took less than two minutes before the first duck died. He remained dispassionate as the rest succumbed. There was no doubt in his mind.

Poison.

Bonnie grimaced. Every bone in her body ached. Her eyelids were heavy, her mouth bitter and dry like it was full of cotton and she couldn't move her left arm and hip. She could hear breathing. Was it hers? No, there were several types of breaths.

She tried to open her eyes. All she saw was darkness in that brief moment. Had she gone blind? No, another attempt to open her eyes caught the faint light of a nearly depleted candle.

She tried to sit up, but still couldn't move her left side. Bonnie finally managed to keep her eyes open and shifted her head to look down. The movement sent shards of lightning through her head and she let out a moan.

There was movement to the side of the bed. "Miss Hodges?" The deep voice came to her.

"I can't move my left side," she whispered.

"That would be Arthur weighin' you down." The Scottish accent was more pronounced than usual.

"My mouth is fuzzy."

"Have some water." His large hand slipped behind her head, his warm, calloused fingers cradling it gently and brought a glass to her lips. She winced at the movement but relished the clean feeling in her mouth. She drank more, feeling more refreshed with every swallow.

"Better?" he asked.

Bonnie nodded. "Henry?"

"In the trundle bed. He's asleep."

"How are they?"

He sighed. "Upset. But fine."

"What happened?"

"You don't recall?" Bonnie shook her head. "The biscuit you ate had been poisoned. Several of them, if not the entire batch. Mrs. Dabbs has rid the kitchen of all her baking supplies as a precaution."

God help her, she almost died. Again. She squeezed her

eyes shut, but couldn't stop the tears. They leaked out and streaked down her cheeks, leaving hot, heavy trails.

"Och, dinna cry, lass." His thumbs brushed away the tears.

She couldn't help it. It had always been a failing of hers to laugh at inappropriate moments. The giggles bubbled up and escaped with her helpless to do anything to stop them.

"Now lass, I promise ye, I will find this bastard and see tha' he niver hurts ye or the bairns agin."

His speech made her laugh even harder.

"Lass, are ye well?"

Bonnie waved her hand in front of her face. "I'm sorry," she gasped.

"Och lass, niver apologize fer bein' scarrit. 'Taint a weakness."

"No, it's not that."

"Then wha' 'tis it? I'll do whate'er ye ask of me."

She gained control of herself and looked at him. He looked tired and haggard, dark whiskers shadowing his jawline. His dark hair, usually well kept, was scattered and mussed, falling over his brow and around his ears. Bonnie's fingers ached to run through his hair, to learn the texture of it.

She smiled at him. "Did you know that your accent becomes more obvious when you're upset?"

Sir Stephen sat up and cleared his throat. "I am not upset." His accent was once more under control.

"When was the last time you ate? Or slept?"

"Do not concern yourself with me. You are the one who suffered poisoning."

"And you are the one who looks like he suffered poisoning."

"Have you looked in a mirror, lass?"

"Have you?"

Stephen stared at her. Just as their first tea in the kitchen, her laughter took him by surprise. It was inconceivable to him that she was teasing him so soon after such a brush with danger, that she was laughing while looking like Death itself. He sincerely hoped she didn't ask for the mirror he just mentioned.

She was going to be fine. Relief flooded through him. It would take a few days for her to be up on her feet again, but she was going to be fine. This feeling of complete assurance that she would recover so overwhelmed him that he felt he could not be held accountable for his next actions.

Without a thought, he cupped her face and pressed his lips to hers. He swallowed her startled gasp and just kissed her.

There was no finesse. No seduction. Nothing more than a meeting of lips. But it was a kiss that shook him like no other.

Her lips were warm beneath his, their bow shape cushioning his. He could smell her, his nose nestled beside hers, smell the mixture of sleep, sweat, and sweet biscuits that he associated with her.

She didn't pull away. She didn't break the kiss and rebuke him with a slap or otherwise. What she did do was remain still, not breathing for a few moments before releasing a small sigh and leaning into him.

Blood began pumping through his veins with the enthusiasm of a victorious military drum. Stephen moved his lips and felt hers pucker and follow, sending thrills racing through him.

The small hairs on his arms stood up and awareness of her

settled over his skin, enveloping him in a blanket of yearning for the solace this meager kiss promised.

Sweet Mary and Joseph, it was better than he had imagined.

A small moan reached his ears. It didn't quite register that it didn't come either of them until he heard it again accompanied by a shift on the mattress.

They broke the kiss and looked down to see Arthur raising his head, his hair in disarray. He blinked at them several times before rolling on his side and resuming his sleep.

Stephen dropped his hands from Miss Hodges' face as if he was holding them too close to a fire. He stared at her, hard, for several heartbeats before standing and leaving the room without a word.

CHAPTER THIRTEEN

"Try again, Henry." Bonnie smiled at his long-suffering sigh as he turned to the beginning of the reader again. "You need to practice." She was sitting against the headboard while Henry stretched out on his stomach beside her.

"I've already practiced this twice, Miss Hodges. When are you getting out of bed?"

"Well, I am making considerable improvement, so by the end of the week I should be able to sit in the morning room."

"The morning room?"

He sounded so distraught. Bonnie hid a smile. "How have your afternoons been with Sir Stephen?" She tried to keep the question nonchalant. Bonnie hadn't seen him since the day she ate the poisoned biscuit. Since the night of their shared kiss, if she were to be honest, and she did not know what to think.

She was not silly enough to expect an honorable offer or any offer at all. A kiss did not necessitate a drastic change such as that. If that were the case, there would more marriages on the record and fewer prostitutes.

Especially if all kisses were like the one in question. In all of her experience—which admittedly was limited to one—kisses were fraught with sensation. Good heavens, the sensations. She had been lightheaded from the sparks that kiss had sent through her body. The feel of his lips against hers—firm, warm, assured. His calloused hands against her cheeks—capable, gentle, confident.

What had swept her away, however, was inhaling his scent and sharing his breath. His sandalwood cologne had teased its way into her nose, his breath had danced over her skin, sending tingles throughout her body.

But when their breathing had synchronized, even for those brief moments, that was when she felt the magic of the kiss. That was what made her finally understand the starry-eyed look her mother would give her father whenever he returned.

If anything, this experience made her want to see him more. Yes, she knew that nothing could come from this attraction; she was the governess and he was the guardian and that was that. But she did not understand why he kept away from her.

Despite her best intentions, she could not stop that from hurting.

Henry shrugged, the gesture shaking the bed enough to refocus her attention. "Fine."

Bonnie raised her brows. "Fine? That is all you have to say?"

"We see the horses and sit in the study," Henry elaborated with another shrug. "It is not very entertaining."

"I thought you liked horses."

"But I can't do anything when my shoulder hurts. I can't ride, so he's teaching me to oil my saddle and curry Harold. And when we're in the study, all he does is work with Mr. Renard. He tells me some things about the estate, but it's all boring."

Oh dear. Bonnie sighed. "Henry, Sir Stephen is quite busy as your guardian. He has much on his plate." Not to mention unraveling a mystery surrounding who it was who wanted to harm them. "One of the things he is responsible for is preparing you to assume the duties of the viscount. You should be grateful he is taking that responsibility seriously."

Henry didn't answer directly, but began reading from his primer.

Stephen didn't glance up at the knock. "Come in," he bade. It wasn't until the scent that had been imprinted on his senses drifted towards him that he looked up. Bonnie—Miss Hodges—stood before the desk, her face pale and beaded with moisture, her shaking skirts reflecting that of her legs.

He stood abruptly. "You shouldn't be out of bed." He moved around the desk, approaching her.

"I must speak with you, sir." Her voice was thin and breathless.

"This was foolish," he said with severity. He lifted her into his arms and carried her towards the door. She gave a startled shriek. "I'm returning you to your room."

"No, please," she protested. "I must speak with you."

"We can do so in your room."

"Sir!"

With a growl, Stephen turned on his heel and moved to the sofas. He carefully set her down close to the fire, ensuring she was comfortable against the cushions. "Are you warm enough? Do you need a shawl or a blanket?"

"I am fine."

Her voice was still too thin. He grabbed the throw from the back of the sofa and tucked it around her legs. Taking care to secure it, he found his hands lingering on her hips. They were soft and supple, filling his hands until they were burning with need to remove her skirts and petticoats and feel her flesh beneath his.

Stephen tightened his fingers for a brief moment before forcing himself to release her. He stepped back and cleared his throat. "The boys are asleep?" he inquired. "Would you care for tea or something to eat?"

"I am fine, sir."

"You are certain?"

She gave a small smile. "You are being quite solicitous."

"You could have died. You are not yet fully recovered."

"We haven't seen each other in four days. How are you certain I am not yet fully recovered?"

Was she serious? "You were on the verge of collapsing on the carpet a moment ago. I assume that was from the effort of walking from your room."

She smiled again. "I forgot your ability for deduction."

Lord, but he could get used to having her smile at him. Even though there was nothing coy, nothing seductive, nothing knowing to it, having that smile directed at him was potent.

Stephen sat on the opposite sofa, sitting back and crossing his legs. "You said you needed to speak with me."

It was fascinating how she could shift into formality so quickly and effortlessly. He appreciated that ability; it made it easier to remember their respective positions.

"Yes. It has to do with your afternoons with Henry. He tells me that you are educating him in the management of the estate."

"Aye."

"Do you not think him too young for that?"

"I do not."

"It is merely that I am concerned for him. He is not finding it . . . *entertaining* is the word he used."

Stephen smiled. "Running an estate is a responsibility and a necessity, not entertainment."

Bonnie suppressed the warmth that tingled over her skin at his smile. "An eight-year-old boy does not understand that."

"He is the viscount. He needs to be prepared for this responsibility. It is too easy to take for granted things inherited and not earned."

"I agree but—"

"Then perhaps you would accord me the respect of knowing what I am doing."

Bonnie had never enjoyed being interrupted, let alone condescended to. Her tolerance had increased out of necessity in her line of work, but this was one of the times where her patience ran thin. A handsome face and appealing accent were no excuse for lack of manners.

"And please sir, accord me the respect of knowing what I am doing as well."

Sir Stephen blinked at her sharp tone. "Of course I do."

"Then understand that I know eight-year-old boys. I

am not disputing the importance of what he needs to learn. What I am questioning is your methodology."

"My methodology?"

Bonnie softened her tone. "I know young boys and I know teaching, sir. Henry is not unaware he is the viscount. He may not fully understand what that entails, but he is not ignorant."

"Then what is wrong with my methodology, if he is not ignorant?"

Bonnie smiled. "He is still only eight years old. Having him sit in a chair and observe conversations between you and Mr. Renard is out of his depth. Using words and ideas he does not understand will only serve to make him resent being viscount."

Stephen grimaced. "That is the last thing I want to happen." He ran a hand through his hair. "It appears I must rely on your expertise here. What do you suggest?"

Bonnie ignored his inadvertent insult. "He needs to see the relevance of being viscount; he needs to see why it is important. What did your father do to prepare you for your title?"

His body visibly tensed. "My father?"

"I assume you inherited your barony, Sir Stephen. How did your father prepare you to run the family estate?"

He cleared his throat. "It is a landless title."

"Oh. I didn't realize."

He looked away, his mouth in an uncompromising line. Bonnie did not like the way this conversation was going. He had become remote, put a wall up between them, and she didn't know why. Was he ashamed because he was landless? "It matters little if you do not have an estate."

Sir Stephen stood and strode around the table to stand at the fire. Bonnie watched him lean against the mantle, his coat stretching across his muscular back. She couldn't help but stare. If his physical strength was so obvious when he was fully clothed, how much more powerful would he be when he disrobed?

Heat flooded through her at the thought.

"Just tell me what I am to do with Henry."

His voice triggered something unfamiliar in her. Unable to stop herself, Bonnie pushed herself up, the blanket falling to the floor, and moved to where he stood at the fire. Her hand hovered at his shoulder, aching to touch him, but she dropped it when he turned his head towards her.

His brow lowered and he frowned. "You shouldn't be standing."

"That is one of your faults, isn't it?"

"Excuse me?" He turned to face her completely.

"You take on responsibility for others. You care for them."

"I do not."

Bonnie smiled. "Why do you deny it? There is nothing wrong with it."

"You called it a fault. That implies negativity."

"Only if you take on too much and neglect yourself." She reached up and brushed a lock of hair off his forehead. "Who takes care of you?"

Stephen stared at her. "One could say the same about you."

"I am a governess. It is my job to care for others."

He shook his head. "Not like this. Not staying when there's no pay or seeing to traumatized children. Not being poisoned."

"That wasn't your fault."

"Perhaps not, but I can make it better."

She smiled up at him. "How?"

"By getting you back to bed." Stephen easily lifted her again and made his way out of the study.

She gasped when he lifted her. "But Henry—"

"We can talk about Henry tomorrow, Miss Hodges. You need your rest."

"I can at least walk." Not that she really wanted to. It was nice being tucked against his chest, her arm around his shoulders for support. She could experience his strength first hand instead of speculate what was under his coat. She resisted the urge to snuggle into his solid chest.

"Take your own advice. Let me take care of you for the moment."

Well. When he put it like that, how could she refuse?

CHAPTER FOURTEEN

"Is there something I can help you with, sir? You seem perplexed."

Stephen glanced up at Renard. "No." He turned his eyes back to the ledger. The numbers remained the same. The estate was bleeding money through bad investments, ineffective estate upgrades, and general mismanagement.

It wasn't too difficult for Stephen to recognize the mismanagement. It was well-hidden, but with his experience, Stephen knew what to look for; it had taken nearly three years after his father's death to pay off creditors and bring the title back to solvency.

How could George let things come to this? Had Roslyn known? For as long as he could remember, Stephen's mother had known of his father's monetary problems, but those had already been severe by the time he had become aware of them. It disgusted him to know that George was on the brink of doing to Roslyn and his sons the exact same thing Stephen's father had done to him.

How could he not have recognized this in his own friend?

True, he hadn't been to visit in more than four years; the responsibility left to him on his father's death left little time and money to leave Scotland. Surely it hadn't always been like this.

A thought occurred to Stephen and it surprised him that he hadn't thought of it before: He needed to see previous ledgers going back several years. That would give him more of a clue as to what went wrong.

He glanced over at Renard, bent over his work. As much help as the man had been, Stephen still didn't trust him; he was too eager to point out George's mistakes and failings. A man of business needed to be discreet, no matter the circumstances.

He shifted his gaze to the bookcase that held previous ledgers; it held the estate records for the last fifty years. He would have to wait until he was alone in the study; he did not want to raise Renard's suspicions.

"Sir?"

Stephen jerked his head back around to Renard. He raised an eyebrow in response.

"The letter requires your signature."

Without speaking, he took the letter being held out to him and signed it. His mind began to ponder how he could get the man out of the room.

"Sir?"

Another eyebrow raised in response.

"If I may say, you seem distracted this afternoon."

"You may not."

"My apologies, sir." The tall man sat back down at his desk and resumed his work.

With a loud sigh, Stephen stood and moved to the window, taking in the view of the back garden entering winter dormancy. Gray clouds hovered in the sky, threatening to bring the inevitable rain that accompanies the English winter.

He hated this part of investigating, the distrust. Suspecting everyone, questioning every action. That suspicion followed him in his dealings with his father; it had been his steady companion both while the man was alive and after.

He was tired of being suspicious.

Movement caught his eye as two young bodies entered the garden from the drawing room terrace. Henry bounded down the stairs, a ball in his arms. Arthur followed him, his short, pudgy legs struggling to keep up. Their shouts were loud and excited, their scarves tied securely around their necks and coats buttoned.

Coming onto the terrace much more slowly, Miss Hodges appeared in her gray pelisse and pink scarf, her head sporting a matching pink bonnet. Stephen watched as she paused at the top of the terrace stairs and tilted her head back towards the sun. More than a week had passed since the poisoning and this was the first time in his knowledge that she had stepped outside of the manor.

He frowned when he saw Miss Hodges grip the balustrade for support as she gingerly descended the stairs. She still was not strong enough to be walking on her own, especially if she were to chase two young energetic boys.

Stephen spun on his heel. "I am going out, Renard," he said, leaving the study. Shrugging into his jacket, he followed Miss Hodges and the boys out the drawing room terrace and moved quickly to catch up to them.

He did so easily, calling her name. Miss Hodges half turned and he managed to take possession of her arm, slipping it through his. He thought how nicely the weight of her hand felt on his arm.

"You should not be out here," he said.

She glanced up at him. "You have become an expert on what I should or should not do."

"I merely meant that you should not be out here on your own."

"Why not?"

"Henry and Arthur are young and energetic."

"They always have been. That has yet to be a concerning problem."

"You recently suffered poisoning."

"And yet I survived. Perhaps I am stronger than I look."

Stephen stopped and looked at her closely. He thought her still too pale and there was still dark circles under her eyes. "I think you are one of the strongest women I have met."

Her hazel-green eyes widened and a blush spread over her cheeks. She glanced in the direction of the boys and then the manor. "You shouldn't say things like that," she whispered.

One corner of his mouth lifted. "Now you are the expert? Turnabout is fair play. Tell me why and I'll tell you if I agree."

"Sir, you are the guardian and I am the governess. Such sentiments are inappropriate."

Stephen resumed their walk. Henry and Arthur were still in sight, kicking the ball on the lawn. "I assure you, Miss Hodges, I am not normally a gentleman who engages in inappropriate behavior."

"Thank you, sir."

"But I find myself in abnormal circumstances."

"Sir—"

"Indeed I barely recognize myself with all the inappropriate things I am considering these days."

"Sir Stephen, you must stop."

"You still haven't convinced me as to why." Where was this flirtatious manner coming from?

"Because it will make me admit the same thing and we both know how disastrous that would be." Her voice was quiet.

Well. He wasn't expecting that.

"Please," she continued, "can we speak of something else?"

Stephen obliged her. "Henry has a strong kick."

"I think Arthur would as well, if Henry would give him a chance."

Stephen chuckled. "Ah, the nature of boys."

"He seems fully recovered from his fall." Bonnie glanced up at him. "Henry has mentioned returning to his own chamber again."

The ball sailed through the air towards them. Stephen released her momentarily to kick it back towards the boys.

"Uncle Stephen! Come play with us!" Henry yelled.

"I'll join you soon," Stephen called back. "Let Arthur practice. I'll play against the both of you."

"Uncle Stephen?" Bonnie asked when he returned to her.

"I'll lead you to a place to sit." He gestured to a set of benches by the green.

"I am not allowed to play?" she asked, feigning affront. "Are you afraid I might be a better player than you?"

He slanted her a look. "You are visibly wilting after just walking from the manor. You believe you pose a threat?"

Bonnie laughed. "Always."

Stephen helped her sit down and joined her. "There's something I want you to be aware of."

Bonnie noticed the change in his tone. "Yes?"

He pulled out a small writing pad. "I made a timeline of all the incidents that occurred. I started with the bridge collapse and added in everything around that. I've noticed something."

"What is it?"

He showed her his notes. "Before the bridge, incidents were occurring roughly once a month, every three weeks at most. After the bridge, nine weeks passed before Henry's fall. Your poisoning happened a mere seven days after that."

Bonnie looked at him questioning. "So after a two-month absence of incidents, two happen within a week of each other."

"Correct."

"And you are sure these incidents are intentional." She made this a statement, not a question.

"I cannot speak for certain in regards to the incidents prior to the bridge, but I am convinced of the others." He looked at her steadily. "Cut girths and poisoned biscuits are nothing but intentional."

She turned to her gaze to the boys. "Have you come any closer to discovering who is behind this?"

Stephen was saved from answering by Arthur's approach, holding a pair of rocks in his hands. Bonnie automatically opened her hand to take them.

"Here, Mama," Arthur said, dropping the rocks into her hand before turning around to rejoin his brother.

Bonnie stared after him, her stomach falling. *Oh dear heavens.* She blinked and looked at Sir Stephen, meeting his raised brows with hers.

"Mama?" he echoed.

"He spoke," she squeaked out. "We should focus on that, not necessarily what he said."

"Mama?" he repeated.

Bonnie shook her head. "First time he ever called me that." *And hopefully the last.*

He pursed his lips. "Just know that you can't pester me about being Uncle Stephen."

She nodded. "Agreed."

Stephen stood, straightened his coat, and handed his hat for her to hold. "About what we were speaking of a few moments ago? There is something else I want you to be aware of."

"There's more?" Her voice was full of dismay and distress.

He looked at her intently, leaning towards her to rest his hands on the back of the bench, boxing her in between his arms. He put his mouth next to her ear. "I disagree that we would be disastrous."

CHAPTER FIFTEEN

Come for tea in the study this evening. -S

The note was presumptive. Arrogant really. To expect that she would obey such a summons.

Well, she *was* a servant of sorts. It was expected that she obey such a summons.

But theirs didn't feel like a normal master-servant relationship. Which was dangerous. She really ought to treat this as he were a normal master summoning his normal servant to his study.

For tea.

Oh good heavens, she was becoming one of those women who analyze everything about a gentleman they were being courted by.

Which he wasn't. Courting her, that is. Despite his earlier statement, courting her was not an appropriate option. Nor an intelligent one.

So when Bonnie knocked on the study door, she was telling herself that this was not a courtship. She did not want it to be a courtship. He did not want it to be a courtship. Thus, it was not a courtship. It was a master summoning his servant.

For tea. In the study.

She must not, would not make this into more than it was.

Bonnie opened the door at his voice. The familiar warm walnut panels surrounded her as she stepped inside, the fire casting a healthy glow throughout the room.

Sir Stephen wasn't behind the desk as he normally was. Instead he stood up from where he was sitting on the sofa. He smoothed his waistcoat. "Miss Hodges," he greeted, inclining his head. "Please sit."

The man was a lesson in brevity. Bonnie moved around to sit, settling her skirts around her legs before looking up at him. He positioned himself opposite of her.

When he didn't speak, she gestured to the tea tray on the table between them. "Would you like me to pour?"

He nodded. "Please."

She did so, preparing his cup as he liked before seeing to her own. She blew on it to cool it before taking a sip.

"I had Mrs. Dabbs send more biscuits," he said, breaking the silence.

"I am abstaining from biscuits for the time being," she replied with a small smile.

"Understandable."

When he didn't speak again, she prodded him again. "You wished to see me, sir?"

"Did you enjoy your afternoon outside?" he asked.

"Yes, we did. I am glad it did not rain. The boys and I were feeling cooped up."

"I had a good time playing with the boys."

"They enjoyed it as well."

Silence fell between them again. This was not like their other teas. Those times had not been prearranged or heavy with expectations. Those times had not been laden with memories of his lips against hers, of his arms carrying her up the stairs. Those times had not been thick with the desire that he actually would court her.

Bonnie put her teacup down and glanced around the room. "How is the investigation proceeding?"

"You shouldn't concern yourself with that. I will take care of it," he said.

"Respectfully sir, it became my concern when you told me the incidents were intentional. It became my concern when I saw my employers die in front of my eyes. It became my concern when I was poisoned."

Sir Stephen lowered his chin in acknowledgement. "I do not wish to concern you more about this. You should worry about the boys and allow me to continue to investigate the situation."

Bonnie was incredulous. "So you are fine with sharing just enough information to make me concerned for my safety and that of Henry and Arthur, but then deny me that which may very well help me?"

"What do you mean?"

"This afternoon, you showed me your timeline and said that I should be careful as it has been over a week since the last incident."

Stephen was pleased she had given his words such attention. "Aye, I believe that."

"Well, what am I to do, exactly? Taste everything that comes from the kitchen? Check their clothing and bed sheets for razors? Patrol the perimeter for gunmen? Cross the bridges, climb the trees, and jump into the rivers first?"

He didn't answer.

"They are young boys, Sir Stephen. Even when there is not a threat, they are prone to accidents. Or incidents, as you have termed them. They are curious and adventurous and things happen; it is difficult for me in the best of circumstances to ensure their safety and well-being. Asking me to increase my vigilance against an unknown threat using unknown methods to harm us is asking the impossible."

Stephen shifted uncomfortably in his seat, crossing his legs and leaning back against the sofa, resting his arm along the back. "I don't have the information you are seeking."

Bonnie stood and paced around the sofa. "How do you do this? Live with uncertainty and this helpless feeling?"

Stephen stood with her, settling his hands on his hips. "To be honest, this is the first time I've been in such a situation."

He moved to the spirits and poured both of them a portion of Scotch. He pressed a glass into her hand. Bonnie gave him a weak smile. "This is the second time you've given me spirits."

"The situations have called for it."

The intensity of his gaze made her shiver. Bonnie took a sip of her drink to cover it up and moved closer to the fire.

"You are cold," he stated.

She shook her head. "I am fine."

He ignored her and knelt down in front of the fire, laying

more logs in the flames. He stirred them, coaxing the flames. The fresh logs caught and crackled as the fire grew. Bonnie felt the heat grow and envelop her.

Sir Stephen straightened and stared into the fire, lifting his drink from the mantle and sipping it. Bonnie watched his throat work as he swallowed, his Adam's apple bobbing up and down. The flames caressed his skin, giving it a warm glow, highlighting his youth and vitality. Bonnie wanted to press her cheek to his to allow his warmth to seep into her senses, to have his scent surround her again.

She turned and sat back down on the sofa. She knew such thoughts were inappropriate, considering everything. Why could she not stop thinking like this?

A silence fell between them. He didn't seem inclined to break it and Bonnie didn't know what to say. She couldn't put a voice to her salacious thoughts and he obviously did not wish to share anything regarding his investigation.

She put the rest of her drink on the small table and smoothed her skirts over her knees. She couldn't seem to divert her mind away from either the investigation or the man at the fire.

Stephen continued to stare into the fire, his thoughts on the woman behind him. He had had such plans when he invited her for tea. Images of sitting close to her, chatting about whatever it was that men and women talked about when having an intimate tea had hovered in his mind.

What had he been thinking? He had no experience with this; wooing and courting a woman did not come easily to him. Which was the very reason why he limited his interactions with members of the fairer sex to professionals more concerned with the color of his coin than the sound of his words.

But he had to do something, otherwise she would leave thinking he was some degree of mute idiot.

He turned away from the fire and looked at her. She seemed uncomfortable. She was summoned here by him and could not leave without his permission. God, where was the flirtatious chap he had channeled in the afternoon?

Stephen cleared his throat. "You are warmer?"

She nodded. "Yes, thank you."

"I like fires in the evening." Gads, why on earth would he say that?

"Yes, their warmth can be comforting when the weather turns."

At least it was a conversation. "Did your parents sit by the fire in the evenings?"

She didn't answer right away. "Occasionally. Not often."

"Mine never did."

Bonnie stood. "Sir, if you have no need of me—"

"Do you ever wish your life were different?" Stephen blurted out.

Her eyebrows raised. "I beg your pardon?"

Well, in for a penny, in for a pound, no matter how ridiculous he felt with the conversation. But he was desperate to have her stay. "If you could change something about your life, what would it be?"

"I don't understand. Why would I want to change anything?"

Stephen gave a small shrug. "It's not necessarily about wanting to change something, but if you could."

"What is the purpose of this conversation, sir? Is this one of your games again? Are you trying to see if I am unhappy at Darrowgate?"

"No," he said. "No," he repeated more calmly. "It is just a conversation. Shall I go first?"

"Um, please." She lowered herself uncertainly back to the sofa.

"If I could change something, it would be . . . my feet."

Bonnie let out a disbelieving laugh. "Your feet?"

Stephen smiled. "Aye. They are large and ungainly. I am certain that if they were an inch smaller, I would be able to run the wickets better and my boots cheaper to make."

She gave him a smile. "I have not noticed any lack of grace, sir."

"You are being kind."

Taking a moment, Bonnie thought. "If I could change something, it would be my hesitation around horses. It would make transporting myself much easier if I did not have to depend on a coach and driver."

"That can be easily remedied. Why are you hesitant around horses?"

Bonnie shrugged. "I never learned as a child. While my mother had a coach and driver, riding horses were an unnecessary expense."

"Your mother is a widow?"

She turned the subject back to him. "Is there something else you would change?"

"My penmanship. It is horrid. My knuckles were wrapped to the point of bleeding by some of my professors."

"Now that I have noticed. But I am afraid that if you

have not mastered it by now, there is little hope for you." She smiled again.

He gave a mock scowl. "Ouch."

"I would change my hair, if I could."

"Indeed?"

She nodded and patted her coif proudly. "Yes. When it is unbound, it is very unruly. Can barely be controlled when not tied up. I spent hours in the mirror, trying to learn how to control it."

Stephen's throat went dry at the image of her unruly chestnut hair spread over his pristine pillows. Easy for his hands to reach out and his fingers to thread themselves through the wavy locks, feeling them twine around his hand after a bout of passionate lovemaking.

Her voice jerked him out of his erotic thoughts. "Your turn," she said, smiling at him.

Stephen cleared his throat. His mind worked fast to hide his distraction. "Um, if I could change something, it would be my marriage."

She stared at him. "Your marriage?" she squeaked.

"Aye. Or I mean, lack of it. I am not married."

"Oh." Was he mistaken or did he see relief in her pose? "Oh."

"I have never been married," he clarified further. She gave him a weak smile. He couldn't seem to stop himself from talking. "It's not that I have been avoiding it, per se. I have just been waiting for an appropriate time. I won't marry without being able to support a wife. I do not think it is fair to ask a lady to place herself in an uncertain, financially insecure position. Such a sacrifice would not be a foundation for a strong marriage. I want a strong marriage. I believe anything less would be disrespectful to my wife and to myself."

Sweet Mary and Joseph, what drivel was coming out his mouth? He believed every word, but why on earth was he telling her this? Stephen strode back to the Scotch, poured himself another, and downed it in one big gulp, trying to focus on the burn down his throat instead of the absolute ass he was making of himself.

"Your views are admirable," Miss Hodges said to his back. "One doesn't often hear that from gentlemen."

He cleared his throat and turned back to face her. "Don't sell us short. Many men believe as I do. But it seems to be expected for the male of the species to malign matrimony. I am fully convinced that my life will change significantly when I marry."

He felt so deep in the hole he had dug, Stephen thought he would take a risk. "For instance, if we were married, I wouldn't be standing here."

She looked at him in question. "You wouldn't?"

He shook his head. "I would be sitting beside you, like this." He put actions to words and settled on the sofa beside her, not close enough to touch, but he could feel her heat. "I might even sit like this." He stretched his arm along the back of the sofa, his sleeve brushing her shoulders.

Bonnie cleared her throat. He was so close she could smell the sandalwood cologne he wore and tingles radiated along her shoulders where his sleeve brushed them. "Might you?"

"Aye. I imagine many evenings spent like this with my wife, just the two of us."

"What would you do?" Her throat was so dry Bonnie was surprised she could speak.

"Whatever we wanted. Talk, read, play cards, I could finish up work while you embroider or knit or whatever you do. It's not about what we do but rather about spending time together."

Well. "My first impression of you was not that of a romantic."

He gazed at her. "I am not sure I would define myself as a romantic, but more of a realist. Relationships deteriorate if they are not maintained. Speaking vows does not mean one can neglect that which they worked so diligently to obtain."

Well. "I think I would enjoy those evenings," Bonnie said quietly. "If I were your wife, that is."

A small smile played at his lips. "Aye?" She nodded. "If you were my wife, would you object if I did this?" He moved closer so their sides were pressing together.

Oh my. She shook her head.

"And this?" He reached and took her hand in his free one.

She closed her eyes. His fingers were warm around hers, his thumb running over her knuckles comfortingly, seductively. She shook her head.

"And this?"

She almost objected when he released her hand, only to find him cupping her cheek, turning her face towards him. She opened her eyes a crack to see him moving closer to her, his face filling her vision until he was all she saw. She tilted her head and met his lips as they covered hers.

His lips were familiar now, but still so new. They moved against her mouth, slow and confident, their firmness reassuring and arousing. She followed his lead, matching his movements with her own, enjoying the heat of his breath against her skin. Small spirals of pleasure swirled around her mouth and travelled down her throat, settling in her chest. She felt her breasts swell and nipples tighten.

Bonnie gave a little start when she felt his tongue touch her lips. That was interesting. He did it again. Very interesting. When he did it a third time, she opened her mouth and touched her tongue to his. She felt his responding growl vibrate down her neck. The hand that had been caressing her cheek slid along the side of her head, his fingers pushing into her hair, unsettling her coif. She raised her hand to rest on his chest, fingering his lapel.

His tongue slipped into her mouth, touching hers, running along her teeth. She mimicked him, doing the same in his mouth. A surge of power swept through her when she heard him groan.

"Bonnie lass," he moaned before moving and taking her ear into his mouth. One hand moved down her chest, his fingers circling around her breast, teasing her tight nipples. Bonnie shuddered. No man had ever touched her like that before and she knew it was a sensation she could easily become addicted to. She felt a tingling between her legs, followed by wetness. "Bonnie lass," he moaned again. "Let me take you to my room."

Bonnie opened her eyes, reality arriving with a vengeance. He didn't notice her reaction. "If I were your husband," he continued, "we would share the same room."

She pushed on his chest, pulling away. She dropped her head, acutely feeling the lack of contact. Her skin protested at her for ending the connection.

She took a deep breath to steady herself and disengaged

from his embrace. Bonnie stood on shaky legs, fixing her hair back into respectability. He stood as well, adjusting his coat along the front.

She moved towards the door. "You are my employer, sir, nothing more. It is best we remember that." The door closed on her last word.

CHAPTER SIXTEEN

Dearest Claire,

I finally understand my mother and how she could allow herself to give up her position as a governess to be a gentleman's mistress.

Oh Claire, I have never been so tempted before. Men have tried, but this is different. Sir Stephen is different. As much as I tell myself that it is wrong, that nothing can come from it, my body betrays me as soon as I am in close proximity to him. My mind stops working and suddenly I am a slave to my body and what he can do to it.

Bonnie stopped writing and stared at the paper. How could she put all this into words? How could she explain all this to her friend when she didn't even know for certain herself?

Bonnie stared at the paper for several more minutes before crumpling up the letter and throwing it into the nearby fire and pulled out a fresh sheet of paper.

Dearest Louisa,

Forgive me for the brevity of this letter, but I wished to tell you to expect me soon at Ridgestone. I will send more specifics when I have them.

Stephen lifted his head at the sound of the boys' voices coming down the stairs, their governess' voice drifting after them at a more subdued level. Once again it had been several days since he laid eyes on Miss Hodges and those days had moved more slowly than turtles plowing a field.

Her last words to him in the study had shaken him. Was he taking advantage of his authority over Miss Hodges? The thought disgusted him. If it were true, he was the lowliest of men, even worse than his father.

Renard clearing his throat brought him back to the present. Stephen looked at him questioningly.

"Sir, I wanted to assure you of my discretion."

"Discretion?"

"The other day I cleared away the teacups and snifters before the maids or footmen could see them."

Stephen raised his eyebrows.

Renard continued. "I don't think others on staff have noticed. And I will continue to do my best to keep it that way. No one needs to be aware of the relationship you have with Miss Hodges."

Stephen blinked. "Miss Hodges? Why do you think it is her?"

Renard smiled. "Sir, it is unlikely to be anyone else. A maid would have difficulty keeping it quiet and Miss Hodges is an attractive woman. I may be betrothed, but I am still a man. I can still appreciate the sights around me."

Stephen's grip tightened on the quill until he thought it would snap. "Mr. Renard, you presume too much. You are discussing women in my employ and I will not tolerate disrespect."

The man of business swallowed and nodded. "Of course sir. My apologies. I meant no offense."

Stephen watched as Renard resumed his seat and bent over his work. He turned back to the books in front of him and continued taking his discreet notes.

He couldn't deny it anymore. Two things actually. It irked him that he had concluded these things at the same time as it meant he couldn't address one without dealing with the other first.

The first thing was that Miss Hodges—Bonnie, his bonny lass—was more than just a fling to him.

He loved her. It was a simple as that. And it was frustrating that he could not pursue her and his feelings until he dealt with the second thing.

Which was that the evidence of Renard being the perpetrator was mounting. Based on the books, things had started going wrong several months after he was hired. Simple entries seemed skewed, such as costs for planting seeds and various farm implements being entered approximately ten percent over the price; letters from his man of business in Edinburgh confirmed that. And the poor investments Renard had mentioned? Further communication from Edinburgh revealed the companies were false, all leading back to a company owned by one Simon Rees, the same initials as Sylvester Renard.

Inquiries into Rees's history showed that Mr. Rees's grandfather had been valet to the Viscount Darrow fifty years prior, until he had been dismissed for thievery. The current Simon Rees had studied at University of Glasgow, studying engineering, chemistry, and agriculture before finally settling on mathematics. And after graduation, he had simply disappeared.

During which time Sylvester Renard arrived at Darrowgate Hall.

It was clear. Sylvester Renard was Simon Rees, qualified to be both a man of business and man intent to inflict the sort of harm that had befallen the Darrow family.

Stephen looked at Renard, bent industriously over his desk. He looked so . . . normal. Stephen had always assumed that men like that had some sort of noticeable characteristic indicating the mal intent, something like shifty eyes or gnarled knuckles from fighting, anything that gave one a sense of discomfort upon meeting. But Renard, or Rees or whatever his name was, looked normal. The only thing uncomfortable about him was his tendency to overstep his bounds when speaking.

Stephen was uncomfortable with accusing the man based only on circumstantial evidence. He needed solid, irrefutable evidence.

And he needed it fast. Before Renard took another life.

CHAPTER SEVENTEEN

Soft knocking interrupted Bonnie's lovely dream. She and Sir Stephen had been enjoying one of those evenings he had described, except they were both naked. Unfortunately for her dream, his body was blurry below his neck. Not even her ambitious imagination could fill in those gaps.

The knocking persisted, drawing her more into the land of the waking. She rolled over and tried to ignore it.

It didn't stop. "Miss Hodges?" Sir Stephen's voice. "Bonnie?"

Bonnie sat up. Had her dream conjured him up? "Just a moment," she called out in a scratchy voice. She climbed out of bed and pulled on her dressing robe. When she opened her door, she squinted against the light from the candle he was holding. "Sir Stephen? Is something the matter? The boys?"

"They're fine," he assured her. "I apologize for disturbing you so late. I had to speak with you."

"What is it?"

He glanced down the hallway. "May we speak inside?"

Bonnie hesitated. "Ah, yes. Come in." She stepped aside to let him in. Sir Stephen moved by her, taking the door from her hand and closing it. He placed the candle on the wash-stand and turned to face her.

His stillness unnerved her. He just looked at her, his eyes fastened on her face. Bonnie clutched the neck of her dressing robe closed. "You wished to speak with me?"

He blinked and his eyes focused clearly on her. "Aye. My apologies. You were sleeping?"

She smiled. "That generally is what people do at night in the dark." Did he just flush?

Sir Stephen cleared his throat. "I have new information regarding the investigation."

"Oh. Shall I come down to the study? It will be only a moment for me to get dressed."

"No, I do not wish to inconvenience you further. We can do this here." He took a deep breath. "I believe I have discovered who is behind the incidents."

"Who?"

"Mr. Renard."

Bonnie's eyebrows shot up. "Mr. Renard?"

"Aye."

"Why? I mean, how? How do you know?"

"Well, there are many reasons, in fact. First, I believe his real name is Simon Rees."

"I don't understand." She rubbed her forehead.

He took a step towards her. "The important thing to focus on is that he has been discovered and will be apprehended. We all will be safe in a day or two."

"How did you discover all this?"

Sir Stephen smiled. "By examining the books and contacting some people I know. But the hard evidence came from a diary I found in his satchel, outlining everything he had done as well as future plans."

Bonnie turned from him. "I'm sorry, I don't understand."

It was Stephen's turn to be confused. "I just explained. He had written everything down in a diary."

"No, I mean I don't understand how he lived so long among us without us knowing. He's a murderer, for heaven's sake." Bonnie's skin began to itch from her agitation. She rubbed her arms and began to pace.

Stephen could feel her distress; an idiot would be able to. "I didn't mean to cause you alarm."

She turned on him. "How was this not meant to cause me alarm? I may not have liked Mr. Renard, but I trusted him enough to not suspect he was capable of murder."

She was panicking. He needed to calm her. "Bonnie lass, calm down. Take a deep breath and calm down."

"Calm down? There is a murderer in the manor, one who almost killed me, and you are telling me to calm down?"

Stephen grabbed her by the arms, halting her pacing. "You need to stop this."

"What are we going to do, Sir Stephen?" Her eyes were frantic.

"You don't need to concern yourself with this, Bonnie. I have it under control. I have a plan."

She stared at him. "You do?"

He held her gaze steadily. "Aye. I will ensure you and the boys are safe. I will take care of you."

Her green eyes were wide. "You will?"

"Aye."

Bonnie couldn't help herself. He was so intent, so sincere. She stood on her tiptoes, cupped his face and pressed her lips to his. He gave a little jerk of surprise, but his hands tightened on her shoulders, pulling her closer to him.

She pushed her tongue into his mouth, eager to taste him and to have him take away this fear. He met her eagerness, thrusting back.

He plundered her mouth, sweeping and swirling, dancing with her tongue. Her head spun with his skill. His hands released her shoulders and wrapped around her waist, pulling her flush against him. Bonnie wrapped her arms around his neck, not objecting at all to being so close to him.

"Bonnie lass," Stephen muttered against her lips. "Bonnie."

Their lips met again, stopping his words. Stephen drew her bottom lip into his mouth and sucked, enjoying the sound of her moan. Her hands slid underneath his coat, pushing it from his shoulders. He had to release her to allow the garment to fall to the floor and Bonnie took advantage, her fingers fumbling with the buttons of his waistcoat. His hands fell to the tie of her dressing gown, freeing it to join his coat on the floor.

Stephen grabbed her waist again, lifting her off the floor to hold her against him again, their lips coming together. He turned and moved the few steps to her bed.

He took a step back and removed his collar and cravat. Bonnie watched him, watched his skin slowly be revealed, her mouth drying as each inch of bare skin reached her eyes.

Stephen tugged his boots and socks off and untucked his shirt from his trousers, but didn't remove it. He reached up and cupped her neck, his thumbs running down its length, before he leaned down and took her mouth again, gentling from his earlier plundering. Bonnie held his wrists, enjoying his controlled strength.

One hand moved to tug on the ties of her nightgown. The cool air touched her skin before his hand disappeared underneath the material to cup her breast. She broke the kiss to press her forehead into his neck, savoring the warmth of his calloused hand surrounding her breast.

Stephen pressed a lingering kiss to her temple before pulling away slightly. She made a sound of protest, but all he did was lift her arms and pull her nightgown off, tossing it to the pile of clothes in the corner.

It was a novel thing, to be naked in front of a man, to be exposed entirely to his gaze. She saw the appreciation flare in his brown eyes and he licked his lips as his eyes drifted down, taking in her tightening nipples and rounded hips before settling on the curls covering her womanhood. She turned slightly, shifting her legs to give him a better view.

Bonnie smiled when his jaw hung open, so she shifted again. His eyes were fixed on her moving limbs. With a giggle, she raised her arms above her head and spun around, delighting in his obvious desire for her.

"Och, lass," he said with a raspy voice. "Ye are the bonniest I ever did see."

"You are a charmer, aren't you?" she teased, putting her hands on her hips and turning one foot out.

He met her eyes straight on. "Nay. I am a simple, honest mon, lass."

Bonnie stopped her silliness, his words settling in her

chest, warming her. Stephen stepped closer to her, his shirt caressing her bare skin. Placing his hands on her hips, he guided her down to the bed until she was lying on her back, her legs hanging over the side. He knelt in front of her, resting his hands on her knees and opening them, exposing every inch of her to his gaze.

Bonnie stared at the ceiling, nervous breaths filling her with anticipation, not knowing what he was going to do. She jumped when his large hand landed softly on her stomach. He chuckled low, trailing his fingers around her navel. She instinctively raised her hips, the wetness between her legs begging for attention.

But he didn't give it to her right away. His fingers crawled up her ribs to play with her breasts again, teasing and circling her nipples until they were so painfully tight. Her focus was so keen on his hands that she was taken aback when she felt something on her womanhood. She jumped with shock, but the arm he had stretched along her body anchored her to the bed.

Bonnie looked down to see his face buried in her curls. Good heavens, that was his tongue she was feeling. He ran his tongue around her opening before pressing his lips to her and suckling. Her eyes rolled back and her lashes fluttered as heat shot up her body. A choked gasp escaped her.

Stephen continued to lavish attention on her, one hand playing with her breast, his mouth on her mound and his free hand adding to the sensations with his thumb on her nub. Small sounds of appreciation pulsed out of his mouth, much like a man enjoying a meal, and the vibrations just increased her pleasure.

Bonnie's hips moved against her will, undulating against his mouth. She could feel her inner walls tighten to the point of discomfort.

"Sir Stephen," she gasped.

He pulled away slightly, keeping his focus on her mound. "Just Stephen." He switched tactics and pressed his mouth to her nub, moving his fingers and sliding one inside of her.

Bonnie arched her back. Stephen continued his attentions, sliding his finger in and out in a thrusting motion. After several moments he added a second finger. Bonnie could hear her wetness as his fingers slid in and out.

The tightness finally burst. Bonnie cried out as she felt pulses of pleasure contract around his fingers and wash through her body. He nurtured it, coaxing the waves over and over again until her body was completely spent.

Stephen pulled away, gently covering her mound with his hand, caressing it. Bonnie panted from exertion.

"Lie along your bed," he ordered gravely, standing up. Bonnie's limbs felt heavy, but she managed to obey. When her head was on her pillow, she opened her eyes to see him pulling off the remainder of his clothing. The candlelight reflected off his skin, sweat glistening on his body. Her gaze fell on his very obvious desire for her.

Bonnie's eyes widened as she took in his large erection straining towards her. Good heavens, he was beautiful.

Stephen lay down alongside her on the bed, his fingers brushing her hair out of her face. She caressed his lower lip as he shifted over her, nudging her legs open again and settling his hips between them. She smoothed his hair off his forehead and boldly drew his mouth down to hers, cupping his face.

Stephen slid one arm underneath her neck, supporting her head, caressing her cheek with his other one. He shifted closer until he felt his cock press at her opening. His body tensed, his base nature howling at him to claim her, to make her his, but he held himself in check. He kissed her deeply, covering her mouth with his and in one hard thrust entered her.

He swallowed her cry and felt her body instinctively tense underneath him, a reaction to the pain. Stephen held still, allowing her to get used to his intrusion. He lifted his head from their kiss and brushed away a tear with his thumb.

"Well," she said in a small voice. "That was expected yet . . . unexpected."

"I'm sorry, lass."

"I know."

Sweet Mary and Joseph, but having her scalding heat encase him was paradise. Stephen kissed her tenderly before moving inside of her. He stilled again when he heard her sharp inhalation, once again allowing her to get used to him. He repeated the thrust, her reaction lessening each time until he could hear the pleasure coming from her. "Bend your knees," he told her, and when she did, he was able to settle himself even more fully inside of her.

Bonnie immediately saw the advantages to such a position. Pressing her heels into the mattress, she lifted her hips to meet his slow thrust. Their breaths mingled, foreheads pressed together, pants and gasps of increasing desire filling the small room.

Stephen picked up speed, instinct beginning to override his consideration of his partner. Bonnie trailed her hands down his back, fingers sliding easily with the sweat. She reached down and cupped his buttocks, eliciting a sharp growl from him.

His body stiffened. "Och, lass," he groaned into her ear as he gave several short thrusts before she felt a warm heat spread through her pelvis and knew he had spilled his seed in her.

Stephen pressed his forehead to her shoulder, a feeling of vast contentment stealing through his body. Sweet Mary and Joseph. He had no words.

He wasn't able to move for several minutes. When he could lift his head, he looked down at his love and smiled at her, one that she returned. He kissed her tenderly before disengaging from her embrace.

Bonnie inhaled sharply again as he moved out of her, the soreness acute. Without a word, he stood and took the step to the washstand. She listened to the splashing of water and watched his shadow as he cleaned himself of their coupling. He rinsed the cloth off and wrung it out, coming back to the bed to press it against her throbbing mound.

She grimaced at the coldness against her, but it soothed as well. Stephen cleaned her, his touch gentle. His lack of conversation unnerved her. When he was finished, he tossed the cloth back at the washstand and pulled the covers over her, tucking them around her shoulders.

But he didn't join her right away. He used the candle to restart the brazier that had died out at some point, stoking it until Bonnie could feel the heat spreading through the chilled room. He replaced the candle on the washstand and blew it out before returning to the bed. Lifting the covers, he crowded in beside her until he tucked her into his side, giving her another tender kiss.

Moments later she felt his quiet snores rumble through his chest and soon joined him in a satisfied slumber.

CHAPTER EIGHTEEN

Bonnie slowly became aware of being watched. She shifted, turning her face into the warmth cushioning her head, taking a slow, deep breath through her nose. Sandalwood and sweat filled her nostrils and she let out a sigh.

The feeling of being watched did not dissipate. She let out another sigh and opened her eyes. Four brown eyes stared back at her.

Four? She lifted her head and blinked.

The four eyes blinked back at her.

She looked down where she was sleeping. Or rather, on whom.

The four eyes looked down as well. She lifted her gaze and met the eyes.

She cleared her throat as quietly as she could. "Henry, Arthur, go into the nursery, please."

Henry leaned in. "Miss Hodges, Uncle Stephen is in your bed."

"I am aware of that, Henry."

"Mama," Arthur whispered.

"Boys, go into the nursery. I'll be there in a moment." Her voice brooked no argument and the young lords shuffled out.

Bonnie bit her lip and raised her eyes to Sir Stephen's sleeping profile. He looked less contained than when he was awake, his hair rumpled from sleep and his mouth slack. She could see faint lines around his mouth and eyes, showing a history of smiles and laughter that she hadn't yet experienced from him.

Holding her breath, she pushed away from him, separating their bodies. She slid off the bed and tiptoed to her wardrobe. Glancing over her shoulder at the man in her bed, she pulled on her unmentionables and selected a dress, draping it over the chair. She moved to the washstand and used the candlestick to break the thin layer of ice.

"Hm?"

Bonnie glanced back again to find Sir Stephen pushing himself up into a sitting position. He gave her a sleepy look and reached out for her. "Bonnie lass, come here."

She turned away from him and splashed cold water on her face. "You need to leave, sir."

"Soon. Come here."

"It's later than you think. You really must leave now." She pulled her dress on and unraveled her braid, grabbing the brush and raking it through her hair.

The bed creaked as he rose. "Now that's a shame, covering yourself up like that." He moved up behind her, sliding his arms around her waist. "I like you wearing fewer clothes." He nudged his head into her neck, kissing her.

Bonnie flinched away from him. She put down the brush and began tying her hair into an appropriate bun.

"Is it always this cold in here in the morning?" Sir Stephen asked, fingering a loose tendril of her hair. "I will have your brazier restocked with fresh coal. And more than that measly pile. Is that Renard's doing?"

"Sir Stephen—"

"Stephen."

She sat on the chair to lace her boots. "You must leave. The boys are in the nursery. They were in here when I woke and they saw everything."

He chuckled. "I'm starting their education young."

"This is not humorous."

"Bonnie lass, are you upset?"

Bonnie stood and made some final adjustments to her dress and hair. "Regretful is the word I would use, not upset."

"Regretful?"

She faced him for the first time. "You need to leave, Sir Stephen. If the boys are up, then others will be, some for hours already. You will need to be cautious when you go down the stairs."

Sir Stephen stood still, staring at her. After several long moments, he moved to the pile of clothes and pulled on his trousers. "Ye regret wha' happened?"

"I regret our lack of discretion, sir."

He pulled on his shirt and tucked it in. "Ye are quite th' diplomat, lass."

Bonnie didn't reply. His sarcasm bit.

Sir Stephen buttoned his waistcoat and shrugged into his coat. "The boys will be fine. Ye don't need to tell them anythin'." He stuffed his socks and cravat into one of his boots and picked them up.

"I don't need more coal, sir. No special treatment."

"Jus' pretend this dinna happen, aye?" He moved to the door.

"Sir Stephen—"

"Dinna concern yourself, Miss Hodges. I will improve upon my discre'ion." The door closed on his retreating back.

Stephen stood at the study window, staring outside. The gray clouds were increasing, threatening snow, and the trees were blowing in the wind. He could feel the cold through the glass.

He had sent a footman for the magistrate and constable. The other servants he needed had their orders. He had all the evidence lined up. Everything was prepared.

Except for Miss Hodges and the boys.

He had sent a note, but she did not come. He had summoned her via a footman, but she did not come.

She was avoiding him.

And if he were honest with himself, he was glad. He didn't want to see her either.

So he left her alone. He took meager comfort in knowing that she had taken the boys outside, despite the weather. He hoped she kept away long enough for Renard to be removed.

There was a soft knock on the door. "Enter," he called out. Glancing over his shoulder, he saw a maid enter with the tea tray. She placed it on the table between the sofas, curtseyed, and left.

"Ah, damn it," Stephen said when he approached the table.

"Sir?" Renard looked up from his work.

"Mrs. Dabbs sent up two cups with the tray."

"Well, I'm—" Renard was at a loss for words for a moment. "Is it an inconvenience?"

Stephen shook his head. "No. I'm sure she is merely being a sentimental woman. Would you like a cup? I suspect she would be offended if I send back half of an unused tray."

Renard smiled. "Hell hath no fury."

Stephen threw him a commiserating glance. "Indeed."

The other man stood and made his way to the opposing sofa. "I am sure she was merely trying to be considerate. She didn't mean to overstep."

"There is little else that binds men so thoroughly than problems with the fairer sex."

"Indeed." Renard prepared two cups, one according to Stephen's preferences. He put two biscuits on a plate. "Mrs. Dabbs—Betty, if I may, sir—makes the best biscuits I have tasted. I recommend them." He took a generous bite.

Stephen sipped his tea. "The incident with Miss Hodges has made me recently cautious."

"Oh." Renard looked at the biscuit in his hand. "Betty is being cautious as well sir. She is putting the King's Guards to shame at the moment."

"Are you certain it is Mrs. Dabbs' diligence that is giving you confidence?"

"What else could it be?"

Stephen stared into his tea. "You spent some time studying chemistry, did you not?"

"Sir?"

Stephen gave him a direct look. "Chemistry. At the University of Glasgow."

Renard sat back and crossed his legs, taking out his pocket watch to smile at it. "At least you gave me the courtesy of not delaying this."

Stephen raised his brows in questioning surprise. "I beg your pardon?" He blinked to clear the dizziness that had begun to build. Why was he dizzy?

Renard sipped his tea. "I won a scholarship to Glasgow on my own studies and merit. I changed my identity. I managed to be hired to a position of prominence for the title that destroyed my family. I embezzled for years without raising suspicions." He met Stephen's gaze. "Did you really believe you could hide your investigation from me?"

Stephen cleared his throat. "I uh . . ." His mind was feeling slow.

"I mean, you didn't even notice the laudanum I put into your tea." He took another sip of tea, his gaze never wavering.

"Laudanum?" Stephen's throat felt thick.

"Yes." Renard put his teacup down and stood, straightening his coat. "I have no wish to harm you, but I do need time to leave without being pursued."

Stephen's head began to fall back, his limbs slackening.

"Careful," Renard said, taking Stephen's half-full teacup from his increasingly limp hand. "You don't want to make a mess."

Renard moved back to his desk and put some papers into his satchel. "You know, your mistake was underestimating me. That has been the secret of my success for my entire life. People tend to overlook me, which allows me to do what I need to do undetected."

Stephen tried to stand, but only succeeded in falling off

the sofa. Renard stepped over him on his way to the door. "It may best if you simply allow the laudanum to runs its course. I did put in a tad more than usual, but it will not be toxic."

The door closed.

Stephen groaned and rolled over onto his stomach. Dear Lord, he felt as though a large boulder was sitting on his back. With great effort, he pulled his hand up to his mouth and put his fingers in his mouth. Grimacing, he repeated the process until he felt his stomach empty and that he could control his body again.

Sweat glistened on his forehead as he crawled to the door. It took two tries, but he opened the door. "Burdis!" he called out.

The butler came out, saw Stephen on the floor and rushed over with a footman. "Renard? Where did he go?" Stephen demanded.

"He just left, sir."

"Get me to the door."

Burdis and the footman dragged him to the door and opened it up. Stephen saw Renard making his way to the stables.

"Renard!"

The villain turned, saw Stephen, and ran into the stable.

CHAPTER NINETEEN

Bonnie held Arthur's hand, the boy starting to drag.

"Miss Hodges, it is so cold."

"Henry, I'm cold too."

"I'm tired, Mama."

"We're almost home, Arthur. And remember, I am not your mama."

"Why did we have to walk to the town?" Henry whined. "The coach would be warmer. We didn't even do anything there."

Bonnie's level of exasperation was increasing. "Henry, whining is not an appropriate form of communication."

"But Miss Hodges—"

"Henry," she snapped. "I made the decision to walk. I cannot control the weather and we are almost back at the manor. There is not much else I can do."

She had needed to get out the house. She couldn't walk in the corridors without feeling the stares at her back. It didn't matter that whenever she glanced back, no one was there; she felt them all the same.

Contrary to Henry's opinion, the trip to the town had not been for nothing. While there, she had surreptitiously studied the schedule for the posting coach, memorizing the timetable for the coaches going in the direction of Ridgestone.

It was time she left and joined the Governess Club.

Arthur pulled his hand out of hers and sat down. "Mama, I don't wanna walk no more."

"Arthur, we must continue. Sitting on the cold ground is not going to help you get warm."

"Miss Hodges, I'm cold."

Arthur started crying. "Henry, we're almost home. Arthur, stand up." She bent down and tried to pick him up, but he fell onto his back and rolled away.

"You said that before and now the crybaby is slowing us down."

"Henry, that is inappropriate. Arthur, stop crying and stand up."

"Miss Hodges—"

"Henry, I have had enough. Your complaints are not helping me with your brother."

"Why is Mr. Renard riding so fast?"

"What?" She looked up and saw the man riding towards them at a breakneck speed. He was bent over the horse's neck, urging his mount to flat out run.

Dear heavens, Sir Stephen must have confronted him and he managed to escape. Why hadn't he warned her he was going to do so?

"Henry," she said quietly. "Run into the trees. Go where they are thickest."

"Why?"

"Just do it, Henry," she cried. He spun on his heel and did as he was told. Bonnie crouched down to pick up the still protesting Arthur, but he resisted. "Come now, Arthur, we must run."

"No!"

"I'm going to carry you, sweetie. You won't have to walk anymore."

"No!"

Bonnie grasped him under his arms and swung him up. He struggled, making it difficult to carry him, but she held onto him and began to run. Arthur continued to scream.

The thundering hooves grew louder. Bonnie risked a glance behind her to see Renard approaching closer and closer. He had adjusted his course to head straight for them.

"No, Mama, Mama, Mama," Arthur wailed in her ear.

"Hush, Arthur." She tried to soothe him. Her chest was constricting with the effort of running in skirts while carrying a child.

Bonnie couldn't hear anything but the screaming child and pounding hooves; not even her own panicked heartbeat could drown them out. She tried to see where Henry was, but he had thankfully disappeared into the trees.

The horse and rider entered her peripheral vision. Bonnie swung to the side to avoid Renard.

Arthur was jerked out of her arms. One moment he was there, the next he was not. The force of his removal and the proximity of the large running animal threw her to the ground. She raised her head to see the boy hanging in Renard's grip, shock having silenced him.

"No!" Bonnie screamed. She scrambled to her feet and

chased them. Renard lifted Arthur in front of him on the saddle.

"Miss Hodges?" Henry's head popped out of the trees.

"Go to the manor," she shouted at him. "Get Uncle Stephen!" Where was he?

Bonnie crested the hill several minutes after the horse. Looking ahead, she could see Renard approach the new stone bridge. From her vantage point, she could see a coach approaching the bridge from the other side of the river.

The two started crossing the bridge at the same time. The coach, being larger, took up the most of the space; Renard was unable to pass. He reined in the horse, whirling around in a circle. The coach horses slid to a protesting stop. Bonnie could see Renard shouting and gesturing at the coach.

More hooves thundered up behind her. She looked over her shoulder to see Sir Stephen approaching, riding Emperor without a saddle. He blew past her, his gaze intent.

Renard saw him. He shouted again at the coach from which men were exiting. The driver was working on settling the horses, the groom helping him. A footman was riding on the box as well.

When it was clear the coach was not moving, Renard turned to leave the bridge the way he came, but Sir Stephen had reached it, blocking his escape.

Bonnie continued to run, needing to reach Arthur. By the time she had reached the bridge, Sir Stephen had dismounted, leaving Emperor blocking the exit of the bridge.

He commanded. "Put the boy down."

"Mama!" Arthur screamed when he saw Bonnie. She

moved to run to him, but Sir Stephen grabbed her by the waist and pulled her back.

"I am not going to Newgate," Renard said, his voice calm.

"You have murdered a peer of the realm," Sir Stephen said. "There is no escaping it."

"Actually, so long as I have this leverage," he replied, giving Arthur a shake that set him off screaming again, "anything is possible."

"No, please," Bonnie begged. "He's just a child."

"I am not a monster, Montgomery," Renard said. "Allow me to leave unaccosted and I will take the governess to care for the boy. Once I am comfortably free on the continent, I will provide them with safe transport back. I do have the funds to arrange it." He laughed.

"Yes, I'll do it," Bonnie agreed frantically.

"Not a chance," Stephen said over her.

"It is a good exchange, Montgomery," Renard said.

"It is not him you need to speak with." Bonnie recognized Lord Sinclair, the magistrate. "But I assure you I am of the same opinion as Sir Stephen."

"As am I," said Mr. Baldwin, the constable.

"You are outnumbered," Sir Stephen said, advancing slowly towards Renard. He pushed Bonnie behind him.

"But not necessarily outmatched." Renard backed his mount away.

"Just let Arthur go," Bonnie pleaded. "He has done you no harm."

"That is not the issue, dear girl," Renard said in a patronizing tone.

"Bonnie lass, stay out of this," Stephen warned. He didn't take his eyes off Renard, nor did he stop advancing.

"Please," Bonnie repeated.

"See here," Renard said, continuing to back his horse away. "We can come to a suitable compromise, as gentlemen."

Stephen was unrelenting. "How many times do we have to say this? Your release is not an option."

Renard's horse hit the bridge barrier. Renard glanced over his shoulder, panic flickering in his eyes for a moment. Looking back at his confronters, he adjusted his grip on Arthur and hung him over the side, suspending him over the rocks and water at the bottom.

Bonnie's scream was cut off by her heart blocking her throat. Stephen halted, but the magistrate and constable both took several steps towards Renard.

"I will do it," Renard said in a calm voice. "And if you attack me, he will fall. You are in no position to negotiate."

His words were cut off when a crack shattered the air. Before her eyes, Bonnie watched Renard jerk back, a large red hole appearing on his forehead. He fell backwards in his saddle, his arms splayed out. His horse reared and Renard continued his fall, disappearing over the side of the bridge, taking Arthur with him.

CHAPTER TWENTY

Bonnie screamed.

Stephen lunged, partially disappearing over the edge. Bonnie dashed to where he hung, Lord Sinclair and Mr. Baldwin fast approaching from the other side.

Bonnie reached Stephen first. She bent over the side, holding onto his shoulders.

"Pull me up," he said, his voice strained. His fingers were turning white from gripping Arthur's wrist. The boy was swinging slowly, eyes wide with fright, staring up at his rescuer.

Bonnie grasped Sir Stephen under the shoulders and heaved. He barely budged. She tried again with the same result. She was pushed out of the way by Lord Sinclair, who pulled on Sir Stephen with much more success.

As soon as Arthur was safely over the bridge, Bonnie rushed to him and gathered him in her arms, holding him close.

"Mama," Arthur wailed.

"Yes sweetie, Mama's here," she crooned, rocking him

back and forth, rubbing his back. "You're safe now. Everything is fine." She looked at Sir Stephen, who was leaning against the barrier, his chest heaving. Tears of relief spilled down her cheeks as she gave him a grateful look.

"What the hell happened?" he demanded.

The constable waved at his groom, holding a smoking blunderbuss, a guilty look on his face. The groom took a few steps towards Sir Stephen. "Sorry, milord," he said. "I didn't have no idea. I jes' wanted to stop him from hurtin' the lad."

"I will see to him, Sir Stephen," Mr. Baldwin assured him.

Stephen nodded and closed his eyes, leaning his head back against the barrier.

"Is Mr. Renard . . . is he . . ." Bonnie couldn't bring herself to finish the sentence.

Lord Sinclair looked over the barrier, grimaced, and turned back. "Fortunately, yes."

Arthur was calming and Bonnie wanted to get away from the bridge. "Please sir," she addressed Lord Sinclair. "Might I bother you for the use of your coach back to the manor?"

"Hm, of course, of course," the middle-aged man replied. "We ought all to convene there. Statements need to be taken and all that."

"Thank you." Bonnie climbed into the coach, still holding Arthur. Lord Sinclair and Mr. Baldwin joined her. When the coach jerked into motion, she looked out the window and saw Sir Stephen standing beside Emperor.

When she opened the study door to leave, Stephen straightened from the corridor wall on which he was leaning. Lord

Sinclair had wanted to take all their statements separately. Bonnie looked pale and wan. "Are you fine, lass?"

She nodded. "I am simply relieved for it all to be over."

"And the boys?"

"I gave Arthur some laudanum to calm him. He fell asleep before I came down. I left Henry with a maid."

"Good."

Silence fell between them, Stephen staring at her and Bonnie not quite meeting his gaze, twisting her hands nervously.

She swallowed and then spoke. "Sir Stephen, I wished . . . I mean, you . . . thank you, sir, for saving Arthur."

"No thanks are necessary."

"I disagree."

"If it appeases you, you're welcome."

Bonnie nodded. "I should go check on the boys." Stephen took a step to the side, giving her room to pass. She held her skirts away from him so they wouldn't brush his legs. He moved to the study door.

Bonnie paused at the stairs. "Sir Stephen?"

He turned and looked at her questioningly.

"I am glad you are safe as well." She hurried up the stairs.

"Enter," Stephen responded to the knock on the study door. Several days had passed since the Renard scenario had been cleaned up and things were already improving.

Stephen looked up to see Henry and Arthur enter the room, followed by Miss Hodges. His gaze riveted on her, taking in her usual bun and demure dress. She still looked pale and wan.

· He ached to hold her.

Henry came to stand beside the desk, holding a football, while Arthur did not hesitate to climb up onto his lap.

"Good afternoon boys," Stephen said, his voice wry.

"Hullo Uncle Stephen," Arthur replied.

Henry joined in. "We have come to invite you to play with us."

Stephen glanced out at the pouring rain. "The weather does not appear to be in our favor."

"Oh, Miss Hodges allows us to play in the ballroom when it is like this," Henry explained. "My father said that boys need to play and that ballrooms can be replaced. We use potted plants or chairs as wickets."

"More proof that your father was a wise man," Stephen said. He ruffled Arthur's hair. "Shall I be on one team and you two on the other?"

"Yes!" Both boys rushed to the door.

Stephen stood and glanced at Bonnie. "Will you be playing?"

She shook her head. "If it is permissible sir, I would appreciate some personal time."

"Of course. Is there anything you need assistance with?"

"No thank you sir."

"Uncle Stephen, hurry up," Henry shouted from the door.

Stephen gave her a wry smile. "The king commands."

Bonnie smiled and preceded him out of the study. Stephen turned down the hallway, the boys running to meet him. She watched as Arthur grabbed his hand and pulled him towards the ballroom. Henry was chattering excitedly about a new kick he wanted to learn.

She gave a small, sad smile. It was time.

CHAPTER TWENTY-ONE

Stephen cracked open his eyes, squinting against the morning light. He scratched his chest, inhaling deeply and groaning into a stretch. He sat up and blinked, bringing the eight-year-old standing at the foot of his bed into focus.

"Henry?" His voice was thick and gravelly from sleep.

The boy stood stiffly, his hands clasped behind his back, looking every inch an angered lord despite wearing only a nightshirt. His glare radiated fury. "What did you do?"

Stephen racked his brain. "Excuse me?"

"You were supposed to make her stay," Henry accused, his face turning red.

"Who?" Stephen asked.

"I told you I did not want Miss Hodges to go. You were supposed to make her stay."

Stephen rubbed his face. "Miss Hodges is gone? Where?"

"I don't know," Henry ground out. "I went to her room when she was not in the nursery. It is empty."

Stephen threw off his covers and went to pull on a shirt and trousers. He strode to the door and headed to the nursery.

Henry followed him and shouted. "You best get her back, Sir Stephen. You were supposed to make her stay. Get her back!"

Oh bloody hell.

"Bonnie? Bonnie?"

"Hm?" Bonnie looked over at Sara.

"You haven't been listening to a word we said, have you?"

She gave an apologetic smile. "I'm sorry. I haven't been sleeping well. I think it is the new bed; I am not used to such luxury. I am a little worn out."

Sara smiled. "It took a few days for me to get used to the well-maintained mattress as well. There are some benefits to living with the son of a duke." She turned her smile to Claire and Jacob.

He saluted her with his teacup. "Glad to be of service."

Bonnie watched Claire give him an intimate smile and soft squeeze on his hand. It hurt to see that easy familiarity between the newlyweds. It reminded her of her teas with Sir Stephen. And that one night . . .

"You are losing weight as well," Louisa declared.

"Louisa," Sara admonished.

"Am I lying?"

"That is not the point."

"Oh hush, Sara." Louisa returned her critical eye to Bonnie. "Did they cease serving food at Darrowgate?" "It was a trying few months," Bonnie replied. "I suppose I lost my appetite for a good portion of the time."

"Oh, poor dear," Claire sympathized. "I do not know how you managed it."

Bonnie managed a weak smile. "I am simply glad it is behind me." Except at night when she still felt a certain man's lips and the memory of sandalwood drifted over her. "I must admit, it is quite a shock to not have Henry and Arthur to focus on. I had been there for three years."

"It is a change," Sara agreed.

"A positive change," Louisa stated. "Now that the entire Governess Club is here, we can offer a full range of tutoring services. We shall be fully independent of others and be wildly successful at it."

"I am looking forward to it," Bonnie replied. Looking forward to a lifetime filled with students and her friends.

With no Sir Stephen with his intense eyes and dreadfully endearing lack of conversation.

A throat cleared at the door. "Excuse me, Mrs. Knightly."

Claire looked to the butler. "Yes, Greaves?"

"There is a visitor." He offered her a card.

Claire's eyebrows rose. "Send him in, please." The butler bowed out of the door.

"Who is it, my love?" Jacob asked.

The boots clacking on the wooden floor captured the attention of all in the room. Greaves reappeared at the door and announced, "Sir Stephen Montgomery."

Bonnie shot to her feet. What was he doing here? Mercifully, her action was hidden in the others rising as well. Claire held out her hand and said, "Welcome to Ridgestone, Sir Stephen."

He took her hand and bowed over it. "Thank you for receiving me, Mrs. Knightly." He was introduced to the others.

When his eyes met Bonnie's, she felt a jolt to the core of her being, a yearning so strong it nearly crippled her.

"Would you care for some tea, Sir Stephen?" Claire asked when the introductions were complete.

"No, thank you."

"Then how may we help you? You live too far away for our services to be of use to you."

"Forgive my bluntness, Mrs. Knightly, but I would appreciate the opportunity to speak with Miss Hodges alone."

"What for?" Louisa demanded.

"It really is not our business," Sara said, starting to move to the door.

Louisa grabbed her hand and pulled her back. "He may speak freely in front of us. The Governess Club has no secrets."

Sir Stephen turned to Louisa. "Miss Hodges left in rather inauspicious circumstances, Miss Hurst. I wish to discuss it with her."

"Louisa, it is fine," Bonnie said in a quiet voice.

They left, Louisa more grudgingly than the others, her eyes promising retribution should anything befall her friend.

Bonnie remained standing, folding her hands in front of her. She focused her eyes on his cravat.

Sir Stephen turned to her, his hat in his hands. He looked at her for several long moments, in silence of course.

Bonnie refused to speak first. She was no longer in his employ. He had no power over her.

Or so she told herself.

He finally spoke, clearing his throat first. "You are well?"

"Yes, thank you."

"You left without a word. We did not know if you were safe or not."

She looked down at her hands. "I thought it best. I did not want to put the boys through seeing me leave."

"You are in breach of contract."

That surprised her. "Excuse me?"

He pulled out a sheet of paper from his coat pocket. "Your contract states that you must give appropriate notice of resignation, which includes time to find a suitable replacement. You did not do so."

Bonnie's ire raised its head. "Are you here to drag me back in chains, then? To throw me in jail or to force me to return to Darrowgate?"

"No." His voice was quiet. "I would not force you. I have come to ask you to return of your own free will."

She shook her head. "I cannot. As much as I enjoyed being their governess, I cannot." No matter how much she wanted it.

Stephen cleared his throat. "I am not askin' ye to be a governess. I am askin' ye to be my wife."

Bonnie stared at him in shock. He did not actually just say that, did he? "Could you . . ." she squeaked and cleared her throat. "Could you repeat that please?"

"I want ye to be my wife."

"That's what I thought you said," she replied weakly. Good heavens, her legs were numb. She sat down.

"The boys need a mother," he was explaining. He had regained control of his accent. "I am not foolish enough to think we could ever replace their parents, but we can do our best. You already have an established relationship with you and they adore you. They have been inconsolable since you left."

Bonnie found her voice. "You honor me, Sir Stephen, but I cannot."

He was silent for several heartbeats before he asked, "May I ask why?"

"We are not compatible."

"I believe we have already proven that to be false. We enjoy each other socially and intimately."

Bonnie flushed but persevered. "I am a governess and you are a peer."

He dismissed this argument as well. "A lowly peer, one without his own estate. We will not be moving in the lofty circles that may condemn such a match. The difference between us is not so great."

"You are merely feeling guilty over what transpired between us. You are being honorable."

"If that were true, I would have married the first woman I tupped."

Her flush deepened with his crude language. "Is it not enough that I have said no?"

"No." He sat down and crossed his legs, facing her. "I have yet to hear an adequate reason preventing us from marrying."

Bonnie licked her lips. She would have to tell him. It was the one guarantee to make him withdraw his offer. She took a deep breath. "We cannot marry because I am a bastard."

Stephen was silent. Hearing the words out loud put Bonnie into a sort of panic. She couldn't take them back, but she could explain them. "My mother was a governess who became the mistress of her employer. All my life, people have judged me based on my birth and judged my mother as well. That is why I have not told anyone; even my friends do not know. She warned me against falling in with a man. What happened between us was a mistake, but it does not necessitate marriage."

Sir Stephen spoke. "My father was a bastard."

Her eyebrows shot up. "I beg your pardon?"

"My father was a bastard."

She was confused. "But—he was a baron He inherited."

"Yes."

"I don't understand."

Stephen took a deep breath. "His was a legitimate birth, but he was a bastard by nature. He married my mother's money and proceeded to drain it all within the first years of the marriage. He threw it away at gambling and mad schemes. My mother had to scrape by to make ends meet. Every week my father would promise that this next scheme would bring in loads of money, but of course, nothing ever succeeded.

"He was a bastard because he broke promises and failed to meet his responsibilities, thus subjecting his wife and son to genteel poverty. To finish it, he chose to commit suicide rather than face the final round of creditors. My mother died of a fever months later because we could not afford the doctor. I have spent the last three years unraveling the mess my father left. It is the reason why I hadn't been to visit George in so long."

He gave her a direct look. "There are two kinds of bastards in this world, Bonnie lass. I prefer your kind."

Well. She had not expected that, nor the warm flush that filled her body at his words. Her kind of bastard indeed. How could he make it sound like an honor?

Bonnie said, "I still cannot—"

"I heard your arguments," he interrupted. "Will you allow me to speak mine?"

"Of course."

He moved to sit closer to her, his arm resting on the back of the sofa behind her. Bonnie resisted the urge to lean into him as she had in the study at Darrowgate.

"I am a simple man, Bonnie lass. I have never learned the intricacies of relationships with the fairer sex. I cannot give you romance, I cannot give you pretty words. I will try, if that is what you desire, but it is not my forte.

"But I can give you a home, ensure you have enough food and clothing and coal for the winter, and will do the same for our children. I can give you my respect, my fidelity, and my devotion; I firmly believe in marriage vows and will not stray from my wife.

"For what it is worth, I do love you. I am not entirely sure what that means, but I cannot explain how I felt when you left. I do not have the words. I want you, Bonnie lass, I want you in my life in every possibly way I can imagine. My soul aches to have you in my life."

He leaned away from her, removing his arm from the back of the sofa. "That is all I have to offer. If you cannot accept that, if your answer remains no, then I will leave and not bother you again."

Good heavens, there was that warmth in her body again. This time it was everywhere and it was more of a fire than a mere warmth. Her skin tingled as though he had tattooed his words onto her body.

She swallowed. "That was quite verbose for one who lacks in conversation."

"I may fall into a prolonged silence after I leave this room, if only to give my vocal chords a chance to recuperate."

Bonnie looked at him. "Did you mean it, when you said you love me?"

"Aye."

"Well, that is the one argument I cannot refute for I love you too, Sir Stephen."

"Is that so?"

She nodded. "I fully understand when you say your soul aches. I have been in a state of agony since leaving Darrowgate."

He reached out and cupped her face. "I dinna lie to ye, Bonnie lass. I do love ye and want ta wed ye."

She smiled and leaned into his hand. "Your accent makes it all the more convincing."

"Is tha' a yes, then?"

She nodded.

Stephen's face split into a rare grin. "Ye have jus' made three men verra happy indeed."

"Three?"

"Henry and Arthur. They tol' me I mun get ye back for them. They dinna ken tha' I wanted ta bring ye back for myself."

"Sir Stephen—"

"Stephen, lass. Jus' Stephen." His thumb traced her cheek.

"Stephen, would you do something for me?"

"Anythin'."

"Kiss me."

"Aye, lass, I was wantin' ta do tha' since I walked inta the room." Stephen leaned in and obliged her.

"Jacob Knightly, you are incorrigible."

He pressed a finger to his lips. "Shh, I'm listening." He returned his ear to the door.

"I can see that," Claire replied with mild exasperation. "Shouldn't you be giving them some privacy?"

Jacob shot her a look. "Are you telling me you are not curious?"

"No, but I am respectful enough to subdue that curiosity until they are ready to share their news."

He pushed away from the door. "Well, I think they will be sharing their news shortly. Miss Hodges just accepted Sir Stephen's proposal."

"Truly?" Claire rushed to the door and pressed her ear to it. She frowned. "But I can't hear anything."

Jacob took her hand and pulled her away. "That is how I know she accepted."

"What do you—oh!" Claire understood his insinuation. "I see. Well, I do hope they take care to close drapes. I have never been so embarrassed in my life."

They walked away, hand in hand, Jacob's chuckle bouncing off the walls.

Want more of The Governess Club?
There is so much more to come!

PART THREE

Coming Soon

ABOUT THE AUTHOR

ELLIE MACDONALD has held several jobs beginning with the letter T: taxi driver, telemarketer, and, most recently, teacher. She is thankful her interests have shifted to writing instead of taxidermy or tornado chasing. Having traveled to five different continents, she has swum with elephants, scuba dived through coral mazes, visited a leper colony, and climbed waterfalls and windmills, but her favorite place remains Regency England. She currently lives in Ontario, Canada. The Governess Club series is her first published work.

Visit www.AuthorTracker.com for exclusive information on your favorite HarperCollins authors.

Give in to your impulses . . .
Read on for a sneak peek at four brand-new
e-book original tales of romance
from Avon Books.
Available now wherever e-books are sold.

SKIES OF GOLD
THE ETHER CHRONICLES
By Zoë Archer

CRAVE
A BILLIONAIRE BACHELORS CLUB NOVEL
By Monica Murphy

CAN'T HELP FALLING IN LOVE
By Cheryl Harper

THINGS GOOD GIRLS DON'T DO
By Codi Gary

An Excerpt from

SKIES OF GOLD
The Ether Chronicles
by Zoë Archer

The Ether Chronicles continue when
Kalindi MacNeil retreats to a desolate, deserted
island after surviving the devastating enemy
airship attack that obliterated Liverpool. Kali soon
discovers she's not alone. Captain Fletcher Adams,
an elite man/machine hybrid—a Man O' War—
crashed his airship into the deserted island, never
expecting to survive the wreck. But survive he did.

Her heart climbed into her throat. Edging along the gravel-covered base of the hills, she moved slowly onward, telling herself stories of goddesses who'd braved hordes of demons without fear.

Yet she was no goddess. Only a woman, completely on her own.

A shape appeared out of the mists. A large, dark shape. Heading right toward her. It moved noiselessly over the gravel in spite of its size.

She grabbed her revolver, aiming it at the shadow.

It immediately stopped moving. Then it spoke.

"You're not from the Admiralty."

A man. With a deep, rasping voice. As if he hadn't spoken in a long time.

Even through the heavy mist, she saw that he didn't hold up his hands, despite the gun trained on him.

"No," she answered, her mouth dry. "Not the Admiralty." Yet she didn't want to tell him where she *was* from. She had no idea who this stranger was.

"Anyone with you?" he demanded. He spoke with an air of command, as though used to obedience.

Despite the authority in his voice, she kept silent. Telling him she was alone could endanger her. At least she was armed.

He didn't seem to care about the revolver in her hand. He moved closer, emerging from the fog.

Oh, God. He was big. Well over six feet tall, with shoulders as wide as ironclads. His body seemed a collection of hard muscles, knitted together to make the world's most imposing man. He had black hair, longish and wild, as if he hadn't seen a barber in some time, and a thick beard, also in need of trimming. He stood too far away for her to see his eyes, but she could feel his gaze on her, dark and piercing, hyper-vigilant, like a feral animal's.

And he stepped still nearer to her.

"My father was in the army," she said, her voice clipped. She raised her gun. "He was a crack shot. He trained me to be one, too. Stay where you are."

She thought a corner of his mouth edged up in a smile, but the beard hid his expression. "I'd knock that Webley out of your hand before you could pull the trigger."

Words poised on her lips that no man could move that quickly—he was still ten feet away—but those words faded the more she looked at him. His massive hands could likely crush a welder's gas tanks. But more than the raw strength he exuded, a palpable but unseen energy radiated from him, something barely contained.

She couldn't tell whether she was fascinated or terrified. Or both.

"You're doing a poor job of putting me at ease," she answered.

Again, that hint of a smile. "Never said I wanted to put you at ease."

"Not another step," she snapped. Instinctively, she moved back, out of striking distance. But as she did, her left boot caught in the rocks, and she stumbled.

Unseated, the stones tumbled down in a small rockslide. They knocked her down, twisting her leg at an unnatural angle. She sprawled on the ground.

Instantly, the stranger darted forward, a frown of concern between his brows.

She kept the gun pointed at him, despite lying awkwardly upon the rocks. "Back. I'm fine."

"Your leg—"

Her skirts had come up, revealing both her limbs.

The stranger must have been civilized at one point, because he quickly turned his gaze away.

"Go ahead and look," she said. "I gave up on modesty months ago."

He did, and when he saw her leg, he cursed softly. "Mechanical."

An Excerpt from

CRAVE
A BILLIONAIRE BACHELORS CLUB NOVEL
by Monica Murphy

New York Times and *USA Today* bestselling
author Monica Murphy launches her sexy
Billionaire Bachelors Club series with
the story of Archer and Ivy: a lavish bet,
a night of carnal desires, and a forever
they never thought possible . . .

Ivy

"What is this?" I take the wadded-up fabric from his hand, our fingers accidentally brushing, and heat rushes through me at first contact.

"One of my T-shirts." He shrugs those broad shoulders, which are still encased in fine white cotton. "I knew you didn't have anything to wear to . . . bed. Thought I could offer you this."

His eyes darken at the word "bed," and my knees wobble. Good Lord, what this man is doing to me is so completely foreign that I'm not quite sure how to react.

"Um, thanks. I appreciate it." The T-shirt is soft, the fabric thin, as if it's been worn plenty of times, and I have the sudden urge to hold it to my nose and inhale. See if I can somehow smell his scent lingering in the fabric.

The man is clearly turning me into a freak of epic proportions.

"You're welcome." He leans his tall body against the doorframe, looking sleepy and rumpled and way too sexy for words. I want to grab his hand and yank him into my room.

Wait, no I don't. That's a bad, terrible idea.

Liar.

"Is that all then?" I ask, because we don't need to be standing here having this conversation. First, my brother could find us and start in again on what a mistake we are. Second, I'm growing increasingly uncomfortable with the fact that I'm completely naked beneath the robe. Third, I'm still contemplating shedding the robe and showing Archer just how naked I am.

"Yeah. Guess so." His voice is rough, and he pushes away from the doorframe. "Well. Good night."

"Good night," I whisper, but I don't shut the door. I don't move.

Neither does he.

"Ivy…" His voice trails off, and he clears his throat, looking uncomfortable. Which is hot. Oh my God, everything he does is hot, and I decide to give in to my impulses because screw it.

I want him.

Archer

Like an idiot, I can't come up with anything to say. It's like my throat is clogged, and I can hardly force a sound out, what with Ivy standing before me, her long, wavy dark hair tumbling past her shoulders, her slender body engulfed in the thick white robe I keep for guests. The very same type of robe we provide at Hush.

But then she does something so surprising, so amazingly awesome that I'm momentarily dumbfounded by the sight.

Her slender hands go for the belt of the robe, and she undoes it quickly, the fabric parting, revealing bare skin. Completely bare skin.

Holy shit. She's naked. And she just dumped the robe onto the ground, and she's standing motionless in front of me. Again, I must stress, naked.

My mouth drops open, a rough sound coming from low in my throat. Damn, she's gorgeous. All long legs and curvy waist and hips and full breasts topped with pretty pink nipples. I'm completely entranced for a long, agonizing moment. All I can do is gape at her.

"Well, are you just going to stand there and wait for my brother to come back out and find us like this, or are you going to come inside my room?"

An Excerpt from

CAN'T HELP FALLING IN LOVE
by Cheryl Harper

Cheryl Harper returns with another fun, fresh tale from the wacky Elvis-themed Rock'n'Rolla Hotel. Summer's hit Memphis, and things between Tony and Randa are about to heat up. She's hiding something, and he's determined to make her come clean. She may be up to Tony's challenge, but can Randa handle the fire between them?

He pointed at the pool. "Show me what you can do, Miss Captain of the High School Swim Team." Gorgeous pools and cloudless days like this one weren't meant to be wasted, not even by expensive girls who lived in fear of wrinkles.

Randa started to shake her head but changed her mind. He could see the second she decided which face she was going to put on. She ran a teasing finger down his arm, and he fought a shiver. "You've got it, Tony."

She stood beside the lounger and reached up to peel the floppy straw hat off before she shook out her hair. Tony hoped he wouldn't be required to contribute to the conversation. Anything that came out of his mouth this second would sound like, "God, yes. Please, yes. Show me the suit now."

Randa dropped her sunglasses on the hat and slowly unbuttoned the white, long-sleeved, gauzy cover-up before stripping out of it quickly. She let it drop from her fingers—

right onto his lap—and Tony nearly nodded his thanks. His eyes were glued to her. He'd hoped for a bikini. Those hopes were dashed. Instead she wore a pretty conservative one piece that was cut high on the hips and low enough to tease at the V of her breasts. And the rest of her was nothing but perfect, satiny skin. "Still too skinny, Tony?"

He nodded and tore his eyes away from her hips, her tiny waist, and her perfectly sized breasts to watch her face.

Her teasing smile slipped a bit, and he thought he saw honest desire in her eyes. She took an awkward step away from him and then seemed to remember her audience. She turned and glanced over her shoulder before moving to stand at the end of the pool. She executed a flawless shallow dive and made four quick trips up and down the length of the water. He tried to be objective. She was a clean, fast swimmer. But none of that mattered. She could be doggy-paddling and refusing to get her hair wet, and he'd still think she looked amazing. He watched her float around aimlessly for a minute or two before she swam over to the side of the pool.

The sight of her climbing out was unforgettable. Possibly life changing. More than anything he wanted to kiss her, strip her, and take her. With her hair wet and slicked back from her face, he could see teasing, intelligent blue eyes. And her body would bring stronger men than Tony to their knees. It was a damn good thing the sight of a water drop disappearing into the shadow between her breasts had frozen his tongue and nailed his feet to the concrete. He might have embarrassed himself then and there.

Instead he nodded mutely as she slipped into her cover-up and asked, "Meet you in the lobby at four?" He watched her move quickly across the hot concrete in her bare feet and felt the despair of a man who was going shoe-shopping soon.

He didn't want her to burn her feet. Or to be unhappy. Or to be here for anything other than to see the finest Elvis-themed hotel in the world. He wanted her to be a normal girl, maybe one who worked nearby. One he could have met at the bookstore.

He watched Randa pause at the door to the hotel and scan her room key. Before she disappeared inside, she smiled and waved at him over her shoulder. And he and his frozen tongue loosened up enough to say, "Shit." He was in for it. No matter how this turned out, he was going to have regrets. She was here through the weekend. That was enough time to fall under her spell and give up all the hotel's secrets. That would be just about right. From famine to feast to famine again so quick he'd probably lose his mind.

Then again, if he didn't go any further with her, he'd spend unhealthy amounts of time thinking about her wet and half dressed. Probably for the next fifty years. She was like the world's most perfect steak. He couldn't let her go, but eating her would ruin other steak for him.

Eating her? Apparently the brain breakdown had already set in. He shook his head as he grabbed his towel and went to his apartment.

An Excerpt from

THINGS GOOD GIRLS DON'T DO

by Codi Gary

Katie Conners is finished being Rock Canyon's good girl, and, after one too many mojitos, she starts making a list of things a girl like her would never do. When the sexy local tattoo artist finds Katie's list and offers to help her check off a few of the naughtier items, Katie may just wind up breaking the most important rule of all: Good girls *don't* fall in love with bad boys.

She tried to pull away from him, cursing the tingles his warm hand caused. Glaring, she attempted to sound firm, "Let go of me. I'm tired of your games. I don't know why you think it's funny to play with someone's emotions, but I've never done anything to you, and I find it humiliating that you would make fun of me over something I did when I was having a bad day. It makes you a bully, and I want you to leave me alone."

Chase didn't release her, just reached out with his other hand and started to pull her toward him. Her heart pounded as all that mouthwatering muscle drew closer to her and he slipped his arm around her waist. *She* might think Chase was lower than pond scum, but her hormones sure didn't agree.

Katie stopped struggling and tilted her face up just as he said, "I can't do that."

She froze as he let her wrist go and trailed his hand up her arm slowly, making every single cell in her body scream to get closer but a lifetime of good breeding and manners kept reciting: *Good girls don't . . . good girls don't . . .*

Still, the part of her that hadn't been held by a man in a long time wished we would kiss her until her brain shut up.

He didn't kiss her like she wanted him to, though.

Chase ran one hand through her hair and cupped her cheek with the other. "Sweet Katie, the last thing on this earth I'd want to do is upset you, but I have to say, it is really hot to see you all riled up." He slipped his thumb over her bottom lip and continued, "Your mouth purses when someone irritates you and you're trying not to say anything. I've noticed you do that a lot. But your eyes heat up when you're ticked off, and that's hard to miss. Like now."

Katie was holding her breath as she swayed toward him, and he whispered, "Do you know what you want?"

Did she? "Yes." She drifted a little closer, unable to resist him. It was his eyes. No, the way he smiled. Maybe . . .

"Do you know where you want it?"

His words were penetrating the fog of desire, and she blinked at him. "What?"

Sliding his hand from her lip to her shoulder, he asked, "Do you want it here?"

She finally registered what he was asking and said, "I don't want a tattoo."

"Are you sure?" he said teasingly. " 'Cause I have a binder full of things you might like. Of course there are some items we could check off the list that don't involve binders, needles, or tattoos. Let me think . . ."

She needed to move away from him so *she* could think. She took a breath, but that was a mistake. He smelled amazing, and she was so tired of being good all the time. She was thirty years old, and the man she was supposed to spend the rest of her life with had picked someone else. Maybe if she had been more daring and less rigid, Jimmy wouldn't have dumped her. She would never know now. She couldn't change the past, but she could let go now, just this once.

Slipping her arms up around his neck and ignoring his surprised look, she said, "Chase, if you want to kiss me, will you just do it already?"